The Flinkwater Factor

Also by Pete Hautman

Blank Confession

All-In

Rash

Invisible

Godless
(Winner of the National Book Award)

Sweetblood

No Limit

Mr. Was

The Forgetting Machine

The Flinkwater Chronicles

The Flinkwater Factor

A Novel in Five Thrilling Episodes

Pete Hautman

Simon & Schuster Books for Young Readers
New York   London   Toronto   Sydney   New Delhi

SIMON & SCHUSTER BOOKS FOR YOUNG READERS
An imprint of Simon & Schuster Children's Publishing Division
1230 Avenue of the Americas, New York, New York 10020
This book is a work of fiction. Any references to historical events, real people, or real places are used fictitiously. Other names, characters, places, and events are products of the author's imagination, and any resemblance to actual events or places or persons, living or dead, is entirely coincidental.
Text copyright © 2015 by Pete Hautman
Cover illustrations copyright © 2015 by Rayner Alencar
All rights reserved, including the right of reproduction in whole or in part in any form.
SIMON & SCHUSTER BOOKS FOR YOUNG READERS
is a trademark of Simon & Schuster, Inc.
For information about special discounts for bulk purchases, please contact Simon & Schuster Special Sales at 1-866-506-1949 or business@simonandschuster.com.
The Simon & Schuster Speakers Bureau can bring authors to your live event. For more information or to book an event, contact the Simon & Schuster Speakers Bureau at 1-866-248-3049 or visit our website at www.simonspeakers.com.
Also available in a Simon & Schuster Books for Young Readers hardcover edition
Book design by Tom Daly
The text for this book was set in Excelsior LT Std.
Manufactured in the United States of America
0816 OFF
First Simon & Schuster Books for Young Readers paperback edition September 2016
10 9 8 7 6 5 4 3 2 1
The Library of Congress has cataloged the hardcover edition as follows:
Hautman, Pete, 1952-
The Flinkwater factor : a novel in five thrilling episodes / Pete Hautman. — 1st edition.
pages cm
Summary: Thirteen-year-old Ginger investigates a series of weird events taking place in her home town of Flinkwater, Iowa, beginning with people falling into comas while using their computers. Includes notes on inventions mentioned in the text that are science, "sciency," or fantasy.
ISBN 978-1-4814-3251-1 (hardcover)
ISBN 978-1-4814-3252-8 (pbk.)
ISBN 978-1-4814-3253-5 (ebook)
[1. Science fiction. 2. Technology—Fiction. 3. Coma—Fiction. 4. Family life—Iowa—Fiction. 5. Business enterprises—Fiction. 6. Humorous stories.] I. Title.
PZ7.H2887Fli 2015
[Fic]—dc23
2014024674

For my childhood friends

Tom Swift, Pippi Longstocking, Danny Dunn,
and Encyclopedia Brown. We had some fun.

Episode One

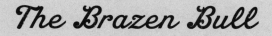

The Brazen Bull

1

Bonked

Most days, Flinkwater, Iowa, is a pretty boring place.

So boring that one boring June afternoon the most non-boring thing I could think of was to stop by Theo Winkleman's to check out his new UltraTab, which was how I discovered the very first person to be bonked by a computer.

Theo's mother greeted me at the door.

"Go right on back, Ginger. Theo hasn't lifted his eyes from that tablet all day. Please tell him that his mother, a flesh-and-blood human being, will be expecting him for supper in half an hour."

I am not a girl who normally makes a habit of visiting boys in their bedrooms. If only because of the boy smell. But as I mentioned, I was bored, and I really did want to see Theo's new ultra-high-rez sixty-centimeter D-Monix tablet.

Josh Stevens, the founder and CEO of

D-Monix, Inc., claimed that the UltraTab image space was so big and so real you could dive right into it. At least that was what he said in the ads. Josh Stevens had been TechTitan's Official #1 Hottie for five years running, so nobody minded much when he exaggerated.

I was thinking of getting one for myself. An UltraTab, not a Josh Stevens.

Theo was propped up on his bed with the UltraTab resting on his belly. His hands were locked on its paper-thin edges, and he was staring deep into the screen, totally entranced. This was perfectly normal for Theo, who had recently turned fourteen—just a few months older than me. He had spent thirteen of those years gazing into one sort of display or another. Mostly playing war games.

I, of course, began to talk. I don't remember what I was saying. I do not always pay close attention to the sound units emerging from my mouth. I figure if I keep talking, eventually I will say something amazing. Possibly something sufficiently amazing to extract Theo from whatever virtual violence he was enjoying at the moment.

I don't know how long I went on, but I finally noticed that Theo had not moved a muscle since I entered the room. Also, there was a string of drool running from the corner of his mouth onto his

Godzilla T-shirt. And the pupils of his eyes had constricted to the size of pinpricks. And he had wet his pants.

That was not normal.

Not even for Theo.

You are probably wondering what Theo was staring at.

I was too, so while Theo's mom was calling 911, I took a peek at his tab. An animated bronze-colored bull was charging back and forth across the display, ramming its horns into the edges of the deep blue image space.

You probably think that's odd, if you don't live in Flinkwater. The Brazen Bulls are our football team. Everybody supports the Bulls, although they almost always lose. Even the pathetic Halibut Haulers kicked our Brazen butts last year.

The animation is the Official Brazen Bull Screenie. Go, Bulls! You can download it free at flinkwaterbrazenbulls.org.

But I wouldn't, if I were you. As I watched the bull bouncing across the screen, I got a creepy feeling behind my eyeballs, like that feeling you get when you see something really disgusting but for some reason you want to keep looking.

I jerked my eyes away.

I never liked that Brazen Bull.

The first thing the paramedics asked after checking Theo's vitals was, "What happened?"

"I don't know," I said. "When I got here he was bonked."

"Bonked?"

"I don't know what else to call it." I pointed at Theo. "What would *you* call it?"

The paramedic looked at the very bonked-looking Theo and shrugged her shoulders.

"Bonked works for me."

Allow me to introduce myself properly. My full name is Guinevere Marie Crump and yes, thank you very much, I know it's a stupid name, which is why everybody except my grandmother Guinevere calls me Ginger, or Gin if you want, even though I do not drink. I am, according to my mother, thirteen going on thirty. Or going on three, if she's in a bad mood.

You might think that thirteen is young for a high school student, but at Flinkwater High the average graduation age is sixteen, so there is really nothing odd about it.

You should also know that I am five feet nine inches tall, I have incredibly lush and glossy reddish-gold hair that hangs halfway down my back, my eyes are bright green, my lips are straight out of a lipstick ad, my complexion is utterly zit free, and I have a body like a swimsuit model.

Okay, I made all that up. You have to watch out for me.

The truth is, except for the excessive curliness of my almost-but-not-quite-red hair, I am mostly invisible. Maybe you think it would be cool to be invisible, and it would be, sometimes. But that's not the kind of invisible I'm talking about. Which is probably why I'm always doing things to get myself in trouble. Because I would rather not be. Invisible, that is.

I don't know why I'm going on about this. If you want to know what I really look like, go to the school website. You will find a truly hideous photo of a scrawny curly-headed mop-top receiving second place in the regional spelling bee. That's me: Ms. Second Place. I missed on the word "floccinaucinihilipilification," if you can believe it. I mean, who doesn't know how to spell floccinaucinihilipilification? I got a red ribbon and a ten-dollar gift certificate for Burger Barn. Definitely *not* worth the trouble of reading the entire stupid dictionary from "aardvark" to "zyzzyra."

Back to Theo Winkleman. I mentioned that he was the first person to be bonked, which of course implies that there was a second. But before I get into that, maybe I should say more about Flinkwater. We are somewhat notorious. Flinkwater, Iowa, is the home of ACPOD, the largest manufacturer of Articulated Computerized Peripheral Devices in the world. If you own a robot, it probably came from Flinkwater.

What's that? You have no robots? Not even a DustBot? Do you do your own vacuuming? Do you mow your lawn yourself? Are you *insane*? What do you do if you have to defuse a bomb?

Okay, so maybe not everybody has a robot. Yet. But just you wait. And while you're sitting in your robot-free household waiting, you might want to consider getting indoor plumbing. And electricity.

Oops. I am being sarcastic again.

The reason I mention ACPOD is because living in Flinkwater means living around large numbers of Very Smart, Very Geeky people. In other words, ACPOD engineers. Flinkwater has engineers the way Addy Gumm's cats have fleas. In fact, ACPOD employs half of Flinkwater's adult population— including Royce and Amanda Crump, my parents.

Do I need to tell you that Very Smart, Very Geeky parents produce Very Smart, Very Geeky kids?

2

J.G.

The second kid to get bonked was Johnston George. That's not backward—it's his real name. Everybody calls him J.G., and he is—or rather *was*—a psychotic monster. At least that's how I thought of him. Instead of spending his free time playing hyperviolent video games like most boys, J.G. went out and performed actual acts of physical violence, like tying a string of firecrackers to Barney's tail. Barney is my cat. I will never forgive J.G. for that and neither will Barney. Also, J.G. once put a live rat snake in Myke Duchakis's locker.

You may wonder why J.G. was not in jail. Others have pondered that same question. According to my mother, it's because his father is the president of ACPOD. That's right—J.G. was the son of George G. George. If you are wondering

what George G. George's middle initial stands for, I
will give you one guess.

According to the browsing history on his tablet, J.G. had recently been perusing a site specializ-
ing in X-rated manga. I do not wish to know more.
But by the time J.G.'s mom found him drooling over
his tablet, the screen displayed only the bouncing
Brazen Bull.

This happened just a few hours after I had
discovered the comatose Theo Winkleman. By midnight, thirteen more Flinkwater High students, one
teacher, and five ACPOD engineers had bonked.

The doctors at the Gilbert Bates Medical Center
quickly realized they had an epidemic on their
hands. They attributed it to illegal drugs, food poi-
soning, mass hysteria, or allergies, until one of the
paramedics pointed out that every single coma
patient had been staring into his or her computer
screen.

The doctors dubbed the affliction *Spontaneous
Computer-Induced Catatonia*. SCIC for short.

I have noticed that people like to know the names of
things. It gives them the illusion that they have some
control over it. Whatever "it" is. I have observed this
phenomenon in old Addy Gumm, who is passionate
about cats, birds, and little else. One day while I was

visiting her, she spotted a small russet-colored bird at her feeder and became extremely agitated. This was a bird she did not know! She paged frantically through her bird books until she found a picture of a fox sparrow. As soon as she was able to attach a name to the bird, she relaxed. The bird was hers.

Similarly, once the doctors came up with the name SCIC, everybody sort of relaxed. Now they had a name for it, and they could set about discovering a cure.

They failed.

3

My Father

The next morning, George G. George, father of the infamous J.G., called. My dad took the call on the kitchen screen. George George's big square face looked out over our breakfast table.

"Crump! I've got seventeen comatose engineers, Crump! My son is a vegetable! I want you to find out what's going on! I want answers and I want them now! Do your job, Crump!"

My father, the Director of Cyber-Security Services for ACPOD, objected, saying, "George, this would seem to be a medical issue, not a cyber-security matter."

"The doctors think it might be a virus!" George G. George said. "You do viruses!"

"I do *computer* viruses," said my father.

"A virus is a virus!" said George G. George. "My son was on his computer when he was afflicted. Find it! Fix it!" George G. George was an executive, not an engineer. In his own way, he was just as much a bully as his son J.G.

Of course one of the first things my dad did was find out exactly what the victims had been doing on their computers when they bonked. I found him in the backyard staring into his phone while riding around in circles on his WheelBot—a self-propelled, gyroscopically-controlled unicycle manufactured, naturally, by ACPOD. This was my father's version of "exercise." Barney was sitting on the patio, twitching his tail, watching.

"What's he looking at?" I asked Barney.

My dad overheard that. "A list of sites the SCIC victims were visiting," he said without stopping or looking up. "The only thing they all have in common is that ridiculous screen saver."

"Are you talking about the Brazen Bull?" I asked as he rolled away from me.

"Precisely."

"It's not a *screen saver*, Dad. It's a *screenie*!"

Modern displays, as I'm sure you are aware, have not been subject to "burn-in" since the last millennium. Calling a screenie a "screen saver" is like calling your refrigerator an "ice box."

"Screenie, screen saver, whatever—it's *still* ridiculous," said my father.

He had rolled all the way to the other side of

the backyard, so I raised my voice. "If it's ridiculous, how come everybody uses it?" Actually, I agreed with him about the bull—I had disabled it on my own tab—but I like to argue.

The WheelBot brought him back around. "Ridiculous or not, I don't see how that bull animation could cause SCIC. But we're taking a closer look at it just the same." He rolled off for another lap as Barney and I went back into the house to check out the contents of the ice box.

I mean, *refrigerator*.

I figured my dad and the ACPOD engineers could handle a plague of comas. This was Flinkwater after all. Half of them were certified geniuses, and the other half were even smarter. There had to be enough wide-awake geniuses left to solve a little thing like this. I wasn't really too worried.

But I should have been. Worried, that is.

4

My Mother

Josh Stevens was once again featured on the splash page of the TechTitan site. I was eating a peanut butter and pickle sandwich while admiring his chiseled features on my tablet when my mom got home from work. She looked at Josh's image and said, with a disdainful sniff, "You can do better."

I don't know if it's ironic or what, but my mother, the formidable Amanda Crump, is the Human Resources Director of ACPOD. That means she's in charge of dealing with people, which is like putting a pit bull in charge of a cat show. I should also mention that she is six feet two inches tall in her spike heels, which is five inches taller than my elegantly compact and slightly rotund father. She is fashion-model thin, with points and edges and projections that give her a forbidding and occasionally alarming presence. Her dye-bottle-black hair is spiky and short, and she has laser beams instead of eyes.

Okay, I exaggerate about the eyes, but she is one scary mom. I am actually quite proud of her.

"Better than what?" I asked.

"Him." She stabbed a red-nailed finger at the image of Josh Stevens.

"Better looking?" I asked.

"He has a pretty face, but looks aren't everything. And he's more than three times your age."

"He's also got about a hundred bazillion dollars," I pointed out. "Besides, you don't know him."

"Don't I?" She gazed at me for a moment with slitted eyes, then seemed to come to a decision. "You're old enough to know this, I suppose. The fact is, I dated Josh a few times."

Nothing she could have said would have shocked me more. I knew that Mom had gone to college at Stanford University at the same time as Josh Stevens and my dad. Even Gilbert Bates, the man who had founded ACPOD, had gone to Stanford. It was a big school.

"Dated?" I squeaked.

"I was young and foolish," she said, "a condition with which you should be intimately familiar."

That's an example of Mom's dry sense of humor. It gets drier.

"Why did he break up with you?" I asked.

She cocked her left eyebrow and fixed her laser-beam eyes on me. I could have sworn I heard a *click*.

"*I*," she said, "broke up with *him*."

"*You* broke up with Josh *Stevens*?"

"Of course," she said, as if breaking up with the Sexiest Man Alive was part of everyone's résumé. "That was before I met your father. Speaking of whom, is he home?"

"I think he's in his study."

She left the kitchen while I munched my sandwich and continued gazing at Josh Stevens. True, he was as old as my parents, and maybe my mom didn't like him, but she didn't like hardly anybody, and Josh had a great smile.

Five seconds later I heard my mother scream.

That was alarming because my mother was not a screamer. A mouse? A mouse would find itself instantly impaled on one of her spike heels. A grizzly bear? My mother would emerge from such an encounter wearing a necklace fashioned from its claws.

I dropped my sandwich and ran down the hall to my father's study. Dad was sitting at his desk in front of his computer, his eyes unfocused, his mouth hanging open, his arms hanging limply at his sides.

"He's bonked," I said.

Mom looked at me, her eyes wide with fear. That scared me even worse than Dad being bonked—I had never seen my mother afraid. She must have seen how much her being scared was scaring me, because one second later she was all business, checking his pulse with one hand while grabbing for her phone with the other. I looked at the screen, and was not at all surprised to see the Brazen Bull bouncing off the sides of Dad's state-of-the-art eighteen-hundred-centimeter D-Monix infinity screen.

My mother can be magnificently unreasonable when she gets disturbed, and I had never seen her so disturbed as this. I almost felt sorry for the person who answered the phone at the Gilbert Bates Medical Center.

"Three *hours*?" she screeched. "Not acceptable! Send an ambulance here right *now!*"

Never mind that hundreds of similar calls were coming in, and that there were only so many paramedics to go around.

"Don't you *dare* tell me to be *reasonable*," my mother said, her red-nailed hand gripping the phone so hard I was sure the plastic casing would shatter. "I am a taxpayer, an ACPOD employee, and a board member of your pathetic excuse for a hospital. Get somebody out here NOW!"

She listened for a moment, breathing hard through her nose.

"Let me speak to your supervisor," she said. "NOW!" Her favorite word: "*Now!*"

I kept looking at my dad. He looked just like Theo Winkleman had, scarily blank and slack faced, except he hadn't wet his pants.

My mother, shooting laser beams out of her eyes and tapping the razor-sharp toe of her needle-heeled shoes on the floor, continued to cut whoever was on the other end of the phone into ribbons with her voice.

Ten minutes later the paramedics arrived.

Mom does have a way of getting things done.

5

The Problem with Engineers

It was a long night. The hospital was crazy, with new SCIC victims showing up one after another. All they could do was line them up in the ER because it was so crowded. My mother and I were asked to leave, but Mom refused to budge from Dad's side. Finally, sometime after midnight, a doctor with dark rings under his bloodshot eyes examined my father and pronounced him bonked. As if we didn't know.

"His vitals are strong," the doctor assured us. "There is no cause for worry."

"No cause for worry?" my mother said. "*Look* at him!"

"I'm sure he'll be fine," the doctor said.

"*Fine?* He's a *vegetable!* I want you to wake him *up! NOW!*"

The doctor shook his head wearily, turned his back, and walked over to the next patient. I thought Mom was going to tackle him, but before she could act, two burly orderlies grabbed her arms and led us out of the hospital, smiling grimly at her demands and threats. They left us out on the sidewalk and stood in the doorway with their arms crossed, making it clear that we would not be allowed back inside.

There was nothing we could do. I thought Mom was about to explode. I mean, *literally*.

The weird thing was that seeing Mom that way helped me keep it together. I was scared to my bones—who wouldn't be? My dad was *gone*. But Mom was freaked out enough for both of us, so instead of freaking out along with her, I got calm.

"Mom," I said, "if Dad were here he'd tell us to go home and get some rest. He'd tell us to let the doctors do their job."

She whirled on me, and for a second I thought I was a goner, but then her face went slack, from rage to despair in the blink of an eye.

"You're right, honey," she said.

We went home.

It took forever to get to sleep. Every time I closed my eyes I saw that Brazen Bull charging back and forth, ramming its golden horns into the boundaries of an imaginary space. Dad had suspected that the bull might have something to do with SCIC, so why would he risk playing the animation? It didn't make sense.

Or did it? Before my father became ACPOD's security chief he was an engineer, and there are two things to know about engineers.

1) Engineers are incredibly smart.

2) Engineers are incredibly stupid.

If you tell an engineer that a building is about to collapse, the first thing he will do is walk straight into the building to figure out why. So naturally, when the ACPOD engineers heard about SCIC, they all got on their computers to check it out.

I fell asleep and dreamed of Brazen Bulls.

The next morning I found a note on the kitchen counter. Mom had gone back to the hospital to terrorize the doctors. No surprise there. I made myself a bowl of cereal and activated my tab. What I saw— or rather what I didn't see—was the worst thing I could possibly imagine.

The nets were down.

6

WWGBD?

A plague of mysterious comas is one thing. And having my dad bonked was even scarier. But losing net access was like taking away the air. I tried every way I knew to get online—checking out every potential cell signal and satellite I could find. Everything was blocked or disabled. I couldn't even send a text.

I ticked off every possibility I could think of. Electromagnetic pulse from a nuclear attack? No, because my tab still worked—I just couldn't get a signal. Alien invasion? I looked out the window, but saw no mother ship hovering in the sky. The apocalypse? Probably not.

I watched as several of our neighbors, deprived of net access, emerged from their doorways, blinking molelike in the bright morning sun. A black SUV with tinted windows and a microwave disk mounted on its roof rolled slowly past our house. A minute later a second black SUV drove by.

Or it might have been the same one.

I said to myself, "WWGBD?"

What Would Gilbert Bates Do?

Gilbert Bates, the legendary founder of ACPOD, was possibly the Smartest Person in the Universe. He had successfully hacked the CIA, Google, and the Swiss Financial Authority while still in high school. He got caught, of course, but while serving his three-year prison sentence, he invented the first functional AI-neurological interface, perfected the graphene logic chip, and founded ACPOD.

His only competition for the Smartest Person in the Universe title was the equally amazing Josh Stevens. But Josh was so good-looking I figured Gilbert Bates had to be the smarter of the two. Okay, maybe I was prejudiced, because without Gilbert Bates the town of Flinkwater would be just another sleepy little dot on the Iowa map. We would hardly exist without him.

Although lately we *had* been. Without him, I mean.

Gilbert Bates had not been seen for a decade. He had disappeared mysteriously after one of the most tragic events in Flinkwater history.

• • •

I don't actually remember this—I was just a toddler at the time—but every kid in Flinkwater had been told the story of Gilbert Bates's three-year-old son, Nigel, who had wandered off alone into the woods behind the Bates property. The woods were part of Flinkwater Park, a three-thousand-acre wildlife refuge between the town and the Raccoona River. Hundreds of volunteers joined the hunt for young Nigel. After days of searching, one of the boy's shoes was discovered washed up along the west bank of the river. No other trace of Nigel was ever found.

The boy was assumed to have drowned, and after a week the search was called off. Gilbert Bates's wife Jenny, consumed by guilt and loss, continued to spend her days wandering alone through the park until one cold November day she threw herself into the gray waters of the Raccoona to join her lost son Nigel.

Gilbert Bates, bereft over the loss of his family, sank into a deep depression.

A few weeks later his secretary found a note on his desktop:

Offline until further notice. —GB

No one had seen him since. Occasionally someone claiming to be Gilbert Bates would communicate with the ACPOD board through an attorney.

No one knew for sure if it was really him. Some said he was relaxing on a tropical beach. Others claimed he was dead. But every day, when confronted with a difficult problem, ACPOD engineers asked themselves, "What would Gilbert Bates do?" or WWGBD for short.

WWGBD?

What *would* Gilbert Bates do if he were suddenly and inexplicably deprived of net access?

He would get back online no matter what. I thought extra hard for several seconds, then went to the pantry and grabbed a can of mackerel. Barney abandoned the DustBot he had been pursuing and bounded over to me.

"Sorry, Barn," I said. "No fish for you." I offered him a scoop of kibble to keep him happy. He sniffed the dry food, gave me a scathing look, and went back to stalking the DustBot.

7

Addy Gumm

Mackerel in hand, I grabbed my dad's WheelBot and rode it up Bates Avenue to Addy Gumm's bungalow—one of the twenty or thirty aging houses in the old, pre-ACPOD part of town. Addy's house stood out. It hadn't been painted in thirty years, and the aroma of cat urine wafted from every crevice. I parked the WheelBot next to her mailbox and followed the broken concrete path up to her house.

The door opened the moment I stepped onto the porch. Addy doesn't get many visitors. She had probably been watching out the window. I was rewarded by her dazzling yellow smile and an appalling cloud of cat stink.

"Ginger Crump! This *is* a surprise!"

"Hey, Addy," I said, holding out the can of mackerel. "I found this in the parking lot at the

Save-a-Lot. It must have fallen out of somebody's cart when they were loading groceries into their car."

Addy frowned at the can in my hand. "That's awful!" she said. "I wonder if we could find the rightful owner?"

"'Fraid not," I said. "I asked everywhere. There's just no way we could ever track them down. I thought your kitties might enjoy it."

"Oh dear. Well, I suppose, if you're sure. But if you find out who lost it, please let me know. I would insist on paying for it!"

Addy Gumm would never accept charity from anyone.

I looked past her into the living room. "Speaking of kitties, where are they?"

"Oh, I herded them all out back. They do get to be a bit much sometimes."

"How many do you have now?"

"Twenty-seven. I think."

Addy Gumm is considered by most Flinkwater residents to be a local embarrassment. Crazy Addy the Cat Lady, they call her. Several times a year she is visited by Animal Control, seeking an excuse to euthanize her pets and put her away in an institution. So far Addy has outsmarted them by obeying every local ordinance to the letter. There are no laws against owning twenty-seven cats, so long as they remain on the property and are well cared for.

Her place *does* reek a bit, I admit.

But here's what I don't like. Whenever anybody finds themselves with a cat they don't want because they're allergic, or they and the cat don't see eye to eye on feeding times, door openings, et cetera, or they just can't stand it . . . they dump the cat at Addy's.

I love Flinkwater, and, with a handful of exceptions, I love the people who live here. Unfortunately, some of them can be quite hypocritical.

While Addy went out back to feed the mackerel to her cats, I went to work.

Back in the Dark Ages people used copperwire "telephone lines" for audio communication. It was as inefficient as traveling to China by rowboat, but it worked. Of course, these days everything is fiber optic or wireless, but there are still a few oldsters from the previous millennium who have phones attached to the wall by wires.

One such person was Addy Gumm.

I sat down next to her ancient telephone and picked up the handset. It was about the size of my forearm and attached to the base by a long, curly cord. I put it to my ear. At first I heard nothing, then I figured out I was holding it upside down. Once I got

it switched around so the cord came out of the bottom of the handset, I heard a buzzing sound. It was
working! I next tried to figure out how to place a call.

Instead of buttons Addy's phone had a clear
plastic disk with holes cut in it. I tried poking my
fingers into the holes. That didn't work. I swiped my
hand across the dial. It moved a little. I grabbed it
around the edge and twisted it, like opening a jar. It
wouldn't go to the left, only to the right. I turned it
all the way, then let go. After a few clicks, I heard a
ring. A second later, a woman's voice said, "Operator."

"Operator?" I said.

"Operator," the voice repeated.

This is one of the reasons I do not like making voice calls. I prefer a menu that gives me spe-
cific choices, not a disembodied voice that offers
a single, cryptic word to which there is no logical
response. I was about to disconnect in frustration
when the voice said, "Can I help you?"

"Yes!" I said, then waited for the next prompt.
It took a few seconds. I could hear the cats yowling
as Addy distributed the mackerel.

"How can I help you?" the voice inquired.

"Can you connect me?"

"What number, please?"

I gave her the number of the smartest person I
know outside of Flinkwater.

• • •

Uncle Ashton lives in Florida, way back in the Everglades. Ashton used to work for the CIA. He claims he was just a "pencil-pushing bureaucrat." But I think he was a spy. These days he never leaves the swamp—just hangs out with the alligators and cottonmouths and his collection of guns and his computers. "Keeping an eye on things," he likes to say. Mom says he's paranoid, but he knows everything about *everything*. That's why I called him.

He answered on the first ring with a booming "Hello!"

"Uncle Ashton? It's Ginger."

"Ginger!" His voice made the handset vibrate. "Y'all got out!"

"Out?" I said, holding the phone away from my ear. "Out of where?"

"Flinkwater! Y'all know they bubbled y'all, right?"

"Huh?" I said. "They? Who? They did *what*?"

"The gummint, baby! Department of Homeland Security. Ain't nobody or nothin' allowed in or out of Flinkwater, not even a text. They got the place tied up tighter 'n a possum stuck in a squirrel hole."

Uncle Ashton talks like a backwoods redneck,

but Mom says it's just his shtick. Ashton grew up in Chicago.

"Did your folks get out too?" he asked.

"Actually, we're all still here. I'm calling from Addy Gumm's landline."

I thought the handset would shatter from his laughter.

"Landline! Bunch a morons! Shut down all the high-tech communication and forgot about axing the landlines!"

"Why did they bubble us, Uncle Ashton?"

"They're saying it's some sort of security issue. No details. Y'all okay?"

I told him about all the bonking. He asked me a few questions, then said, "This is bad, baby. ACPOD is one of the government's most important contractors. They provide all the AI interfaces and most of the smart chips for everything from IRS auditors to peacekeeper drones. Not to mention the hundred thousand SpyBots the DHS goes through every year. If somebody's attacking ACPOD, ain't no wonder Homeland Security's barkin' like a blue-tick hound up a tree full of wildcats. Maybe this'll scare Gilbert Bates out from whatever badger hole he's been hiding in for the past ten years."

"Unless he got bonked too."

"Far as I can tell, it's happening only in Flinkwater, baby. The rest of the world is bonk free. Even so, I bet Josh Stevens is having a big fat Holstein cow right about now."

"Josh Stevens? Why?"

"Because D-Monix makes three quarters of the tabs and desktops sold in this country. If people are being attacked by their computers, it could kick his business in the you know what."

"I don't think it's the computers doing the bonking, Uncle Ashton. I think it's the Brazen Bull."

There was a moment of silence.

"Tell me about this bull, punkin."

"Everybody who got bonked had the same thing on their screen." I told him about the Brazen Bull and how I'd discovered the very first bonk victim.

"Hmmm. But if everybody's using the same screenie, that don't prove nothin'. That ol' bull pops up automatic-like a minute or so after you stop punchin' buttons, right?"

"Yeah, but *I* didn't bonk, and I have my screenie disabled. And everybody who got bonked had the bull playing."

"Yes, but you told me you looked at the bull when it was playing on your friend's computer, and you seem to be okay. Does your mom have this Brazen Bull on her computer?"

"Um, yeah, I think so."

"And she *didn't* bonk, right?"

"Maybe some people are more bonkable."

"Or maybe it's not just the bull doing the bonking."

"What should I do, Uncle Ashton?"

"First, just to be on the safe side, stay away from that dang bull. Second—"

Click.

That was it. The phone had gone dead. Apparently there was at least one nonmoron working for Homeland Security.

8

Bubbled

After leaving Addy's, I took a ride around town. Uncle Ashton was right. We were bubbled. Not an actual bubble of course, but the roads were blocked, and a bunch of men and women wearing dark gray uniforms were erecting a twelve-foot-tall razor-wire fence all around the edge of town. It looked like a war zone. And if Uncle Ashton was right, maybe we *were* under attack.

I talked to a few dazed-looking citizens and learned some things.

First, the SCIC plague had bonked half the ACPOD engineering staff. The hospital was getting full, so they were putting new patients on cots in the high school gymnasium. Second, all computer use in Flinkwater had been banned, and Homeland Security was going door-to-door

confiscating tabs and desktops. Third, no one was
allowed to leave Flinkwater until a cause and cure
for SCIC were discovered.

What would Gilbert Bates do?

I got home just as the Homeland Security teams
were starting on our block. I put my tab in a plastic bag and hid it at the bottom of Barney's cat box.
Barney observed this procedure with that disdainful
aloofness that only a purebred Siamese can pull off,
then climbed into the box and delicately deposited
an extremely fragrant gift atop the freshly disturbed
cat litter. He examined his work and pronounced it
satisfactory with a little *merp*.

"Good job," I told him.

My brilliant cat-box ploy turned out to be unneces-
sary. The DHS guys were tired and cranky and didn't
look very hard at all. They took our phones, my dad's
desktop, and an old tab that I hardly used anymore.
I thought they might take our DustBots as well, but
they didn't. I suppose it would have been impracti-
cal, what with just about everybody in Flinkwater
having a dozen of the little things crawling around
the house.

As soon as they left, I dug my tab out of Barney's
cat box, sanitized it with multiple applications of
disinfectant, and got to work. Uncle Ashton had

told me to stay away from the Brazen Bull, but I do not always listen.

Naturally, I took precautions.

I was sitting at my desk wearing mirrored, polarized, Vaseline-smeared sunglasses and listening to some painfully loud static over my headset while watching the Brazen Bull bounce off the sides of my tab when Barney leaped into my lap without warning. Barney will jump on anybody's lap, anywhere, anytime, and more often than not scare the heck out of them. I was used to it. Barney liked to watch videos.

What I was not used to was the horrendous screech that came out of him when he looked at the Brazen Bull.

The screech punched through the static on my headset like a positronium gamma-ray laser through a tar paper shack. It sounded like—well, let me just say that for one endless moment I thought the DHS had nuked us all.

In the same instant Barney executed a vertical leap that took him within inches of the ceiling as I—and my chair—performed a backward somersault terminating in a perfect two-point landing, those two points being my knees and my face.

Painful? Yes. But as soon as I regained my senses, I realized that Barney—who had teleported out of my room the way cats will do—had given me a clue.

The Brazen Bull had done whatever it was that the Brazen Bull did, but I remained unbonked, no doubt due to the protective measures I had taken, i.e., the greased-up glasses and staticky headset. I blacked the screen and saved the recording I had been making.

You see how clever I can be? I had set up the computer to record every instant of Brazen Bull bouncing, and now had a record of the exact moment when it did its cat-freaking people-bonking thing. All I had to do then was play it back, very, very slowly, with my now-proven protective gear in place.

Back in the 1950s there was this guy who claimed that movie theater owners could get people to buy more popcorn if they flashed momentary images of popcorn on the movie screen. He called it "subliminal messaging." The idea was that the moviegoers would not consciously notice the one-twentieth-of-a-second image, but their *sub*conscious would see that tub of delicious popcorn swimming in butter and tell their stomachs to head for the concession stand. Since then lots of sneaky people have tried to get other people to do stuff by using these so-called subliminal messages.

But it doesn't work. Turns out it's one of those

things like perpetual motion. People want so much to believe in it they keep trying and failing.

Only here's the thing: When I played back the Brazen Bull animation, I discovered that someone had succeeded.

What I found, looking at the Brazen Bull in super slow motion, was a high-rez image of Johnston George, aka J.G., wearing a tutu and high heels, his hair in pigtails, sucking on a baby's pacifier, holding a sign reading I AM PATHETIC. In real time the image appeared for only .008 seconds—less time than it takes to blink. That image was followed up 1.66 seconds later by a photo of J.G. with his finger up his nose, then another photo of him squeezing a zit, and several other highly personal and unflattering images I flat out refuse to describe. It was impossible to tell which photos had been doctored and which were real. All of them had a real-time duration of less than one hundredth of a second.

It was a brilliant and horrific collection, and I knew at once who was responsible: my future husband, Billy George.

9

Billy George

Thirteen might seem too young for a girl to begin planning her wedding, but as my mother is fond of pointing out, I am quite precocious. And I do like to plan ahead.

Billy George, my intended, was also precocious, though he was still quite immature—even younger than me, by a full six months. And somewhat short. Which wasn't a big problem, but it would be convenient to have a husband who could reach things on high shelves. My biggest problem was that Billy George was J.G.'s younger brother. I was not looking forward to having a psychotic monster for a brother-in-law, but even that would not deter me. I was in major crush mode with Billy. There, I said it. Right brain talks to left brain. My corpus callosum works just fine, thank you.

Of course, Billy had no idea that we were

destined to be married—a minor detail. Like most boys, he was blissfully unaware of the outside world 99 percent of the time. Including me, for example. Which was unfortunate. But I didn't hold it against him, because with Billy it was nothing personal. He wasn't trying to be rude or mean, he was just focused. Focused as a positronium gamma-ray laser.

I found Billy in his subbasement chamber staring into his desktop display. For a moment I thought he'd bonked, but then his hand twitched, and the image on the screen—a witch with extraordinarily large mammary glands—morphed into some sort of heavily armored warrior god.

Billy was playing Ghast Wars.

I took a few seconds to admire his thick, tousled, dark brown hair. It was the sort of hair that makes you want to get your fingers tangled in it.

I said, "Hey."

Billy did not shift his gaze by so much as a nanometer.

As I do not like being ignored, I stuck my face directly between his face and the screen and stared into his big brown eyes. He had nice lips, too. I imagined what it would be like to kiss them, but I restrained myself. It would be better if it was his idea. Besides, I didn't want him to confuse

me with some big-chested witch-warrior out of
Ghast Wars.

He pushed my head aside, as if I were an inani-
mate intrusion blocking his view. I shoved my own
lovely lips back between him and his object of
fascination and said, rather loudly, "Billy!"

That got him.

"Gin?" he said, blinking rapidly.

"Gin," I agreed.

"What's up?"

"Well," I said, "let's see. The nets are down, my
cat has gone insane, the Department of Homeland
Security is ready to drop a nuke on us any second
now, and half of Flinkwater is bonked."

"Bonked?"

"Comatose. Literally."

"Cool! When did all that happen?"

I grabbed the arms of his chair and rotated
him away from his screen.

"You haven't noticed the twelve-foot-tall
razor-wire fence they're putting up around
Flinkwater?"

"I've been busy."

"What, playing Ghast Wars? For two days
straight?"

"I'm on a roll."

"You didn't notice the men in black going

through your house confiscating all the tabs and desktops?"

"They must have missed *my* room."

That wasn't too surprising. Billy's subbasement room was an old bomb shelter from the last millennium. Easy to miss if you didn't know about the secret stairway at the back of the hall closet.

"I can't believe your parents didn't say anything."

Billy shrugged. "I don't talk to them much. Most of the time my mom's busy with her yoga and exercise classes and school board meetings and charities and whatever else she does. And my dad, well, he's always at work. Being George G. George is like a twenty-four/seven deal. He hardly ever remembers I exist."

"You didn't notice when J.G. bonked yesterday?"

"J.G. bonked?" Billy laughed.

Earlier I mentioned a couple of J.G.'s little pranks, but I neglected to mention his most infamous stunt.

A few weeks back, just before school let out for the summer, Billy George had shown up for class with a nose problem. He had awakened that morning with what he thought was a bad cold—his nose was completely stuffed-up—but he felt okay, so he got dressed and went to school. I happened to notice that things were not right with him, nostri-logically speaking.

"Billy," I said, "your nose has no holes."

"No nodrils, you mea do tay?" he replied stuffily.

The school medic quickly diagnosed the prob-lem. At some point during the night, a person or persons unknown had sneaked into Billy's room with a tube of ethyl 2-cyanoacrylate, applied it to Billy's nostrils, and squeezed his nose shut.

Ethyl 2-cyanoacrylate, in case you don't know, is sometimes called "super glue."

It took two hours for the doctors to laser Billy's nostrils apart, leaving him with a very sore and very red nose for several days thereafter.

Of course, everyone—including Billy—knew who the unknown perpetrator was.

"How is he doing?" Billy asked, still grinning.

"You mean J.G.?" I said.

"Yeah. You said he got bonked."

"He's in the hospital, along with a hundred-some other people."

"Uh"—Billy's smile wavered—"oh."

Something hit me then. Looking past Billy at his computer display, I saw that his Ghast War ava-tars were continuing their game. In other words, he was plugged into the net.

I said, "You're online."

"Well, duh."

"That's impossible. Homeland Security shut down Flinkwater. No wireless, no cellular, no satellite, no nothing. How are you getting a signal?"

"I have my ways."

10

Poopnet

"Remember the last time the nets crashed?" Billy said.

I knew *exactly* what he was talking about. A local pig farmer named Elwin Hogg—I'm not kidding—was excavating a new hog-waste lagoon. You know what goes in a hog-waste lagoon, right? Right. Anyway, Elwin got a little overenthusiastic with his backhoe and sliced right through ACPOD's main cable bundle. That wouldn't have been so bad, except for some unusual sunspot activity that was happening at the same time, which had messed up the satellite reception. For nearly twelve hours the residents of Flinkwater had no Internet.

For a plugged-in kid like Billy George, it was like being dead.

"After that," he said, "I decided to run a wire into Halibut."

Halibut is the closest town to Flinkwater. And before you ask why a town in the middle of landlocked Iowa would be named after an ocean-dwelling flatfish, allow me to share this useless and possibly untrue factoid: Halibut was named after Arnold Halibutt, with two *t*'s, who moved his family to Iowa and founded the town in 1853, then died three years later from something called the bloody flux. Halibutt's grandchildren, tired of having their name and the name of their town misspelled, dropped the extra *t* from both. And by the way, if you do not know what the bloody flux is, consider yourself fortunate. Look it up if you have to, but don't say I didn't warn you.

"You ran a wire into Halibut?" I said.

"I ran a wire into Halibut," Billy said.

"I know. You just said that."

"Then why did you say it like a question?"

"Out of astonishment and disbelief," I said. "Halibut is sixteen miles away!"

"Sixteen point six, actually."

"That's a lot of wire," I said.

Billy rolled his eyes. "I didn't wire it *literally*! I wired it *virtually*."

"I see," I said, as if I had the faintest idea what he was talking about.

"It was simple. Flinkwater and Halibut use the same wastewater treatment facility, so I tapped into the sewer system. I call it Poopnet. It's a little slow, but I'm loading in the sixty-gig range."

"If that's slow, what do you consider *fast*?" I asked. Sixty gigabytes per second is *blazing* fast.

"Well, usually I tap in through the ACPOD servers, and they can go double that."

I was speechless, and that is something that *never* happens. The ACPOD server network is one of the most secure nets on the planet, and Billy had just told me he used it for playing Ghast Wars.

"I wondered why I haven't been able to get access through ACPOD lately," he said.

I found my tongue and put it back to work. "Do you ever emerge from this crypt?"

"Sometimes I go upstairs to eat," he said, and went back to staring into his display. The witch with the big bazooms was back.

Thanks to the Poopnet.

I realized that I was getting off track—after all, I wasn't there to explore Billy's illegal use of the ACPOD network, or his probably even more illegal Poopnet. I was there to solve the mystery of the Brazen Bull and, I hoped, to figure out how to debonk my dad.

Billy had sunk back into his Ghast Wars game. The witch and the warrior were morphing back and forth, casting spells and firing lightning bolts in an effort to break through a mob of slavering zombies. I could see that extreme measures would be required to get his attention, so I knuckle-punched him.

"Ow!" He jerked away from me and clapped a hand to his shoulder. "What was that?"

"Zombie bite," I said. "You're undead now."

He checked his shoulder for signs of broken skin, but I hadn't hit him that hard.

I said, "Billy, we've got a serious problem here, and since it looks like you're the one who caused it, how about you help me figure out how to hit the undo button."

"Okay," he said. "What's the problem?"

Any intelligence test would put Billy George in the top one tenth of 1 percent of geniuses, which I sometimes think is another way of saying "dumb as a stump."

I ticked off several items on my fingers. "One, at last count there were one hundred sixty-two comatose Flinkwater residents in the hospital, which is a hundred sixty-two more than there were two days ago, and the person who caused it is sitting right in front of me. Two, one of the coma victims is my dad. Three, the nets are down. And four, if you don't help me get this whole mess straightened out, I'm going to kick your butt."

Billy thought for a moment, then said, "Is that all?"

"That's not enough?"

"Just checking. I have an idea." He got out of his chair and started digging around in an over-flowing box full of cables and other electronic equipment. It took a while. Finally he came up with a small, squarish object that looked like an old-style cell phone.

"What's that?" I asked.

He pointed it at me, and I recognized it. I snatched up the first thing at hand and threw it at him as hard as I could.

11

Projac

Unfortunately—or fortunately, depending on your point of view—the thing I'd grabbed was a Smart-O-Rang. The Rang sailed straight at Billy's head, rolled right at the last instant, and missed him by several inches before returning to land at its precise original position next to my hand.

Rangs were huge a few years back, when every parent in the country bought one for their kid. The idea was that you could throw them as hard as you wanted at anything and anybody—and the Rang would miss. A safety-conscious parent's dream. Like I said, they sold a bazillion of them, but the fad didn't last on account of it wasn't much fun to throw something that never hit anything— although it was excellent for startling someone who was about to blast you with a ray gun.

"Hey!" Billy said, jumping back.

"Don't *point* that thing at me!" I yelled back at him.

Billy looked at the object in his hand as if he'd forgotten it was there.

"Sorry," he said.

Somehow Billy George had gotten hold of a Projac prototype. I recognized it because my dad had been involved in testing the new weapon.

Sometimes I snoop a little.

A Projac works like an old-fashioned Taser, only instead of shooting out darts attached to wires, it's wireless. You can fire it at somebody up to twenty feet away, and it sends out an electronic pulse, delivering an eighty-thousand-volt shock. Sort of the opposite of a Rang.

"Where'd you get that thing?" I asked.

"Um . . . I found it?"

"Right."

"Seriously. In J.G.'s room. I confiscated it, actually."

"How did J.G. get a top secret weapon proto-type?"

"J.G. is very resourceful. Come on, let's go see him."

"Wait! What do you need the Projac for?"

"I'll explain on the way to the hospital." Billy started up the stairs.

I said, "If you're going to carry that thing

around with you, you'd better put it in your pocket."

"Oh. Okay." Billy jammed the Projac into the front pocket of his jeans. "Let's go."

The streets of Flinkwater were all but deserted. Not that they were ever very busy. Flinkwater residents have always been indoor types. In fact, more than half of ACPOD employees work from home. But as Billy and I walked the ten blocks to the hospital, we saw only two other pedestrians, one squirrel, and four vehicles. Three of those vehicles were black SUVs, the official transport of Homeland Security. I wondered what the penalty would be for possessing a top secret weapon prototype. Fortunately, they ignored us.

Billy had sunk into another one of his zones. Probably replaying his latest Ghast War moves. I punched him on the shoulder again.

"Ow!"

"You were going to tell me what we're doing."

"Oh. Okay. Um . . . you know how you remember exactly where you were the first time you broke a trillion points in IA?"

I never got anywhere *near* a trillion points playing Interzone Apocalypse, but I nodded. I didn't want to interrupt his flow.

"See, there are certain forms of input that go into your head and get stuck. It's not usually good stuff like breaking a trillion. Mostly it's stuff with

a high horror factor. Like, I will never be able to
forget the first time my primary server crashed. It
was one fifty-three a.m. on September seventeenth,
twenty—"

"Billy! Focus!"

"Sorry."

"You're saying that sometimes stuff happens
that you just can't forget?"

"That's what I just said."

"Well, you didn't say that *exactly*."

"I didn't?"

"Never mind. So what's that got to do with all
those people bonking?"

"Well . . . I think it has to do with the WDK
Factor. . . ."

"Oh. Great. The WDK Factor."

12

The WDK Factor

If you don't live in Flinkwater, you might not know about the WDK Factor.

Allow me to explain.

Long before computers, people used a primitive adding machine called an abacus—basically a rack of beads strung on wires. If you wanted to subtract the price of three melons from the value of a goat and add 10 percent due to the goat being pregnant, an abacus was all you needed. But abacuses were not so good for, say, projecting the trajectory of an artillery shell or modeling the turbulence created by a hydroelectric dam. That's why computers were invented.

Computers are, of course, binary. They only know two things: on and off. In a way they are simpler than an abacus, but one heck of a lot faster. Instead of performing a few dozen operations

per minute, they can crank out several gigamega-
quadrazillion. Give or take.

But it wasn't as if some genius one day said,
"Hey! I know! Let's attach a cord to this abacus and
plug it in!" There were several centuries of inter-
mediate steps. In the last few decades those steps
were mostly performed by computers designed by
computers to design better and faster computers.
Skynet here we come! Break out the Terminator
repellent!

Seriously, we won't have to worry about artificial intelligences taking over the planet for at *least*
another fifteen or twenty years.

Give or take.

My point is, we now have several generations
of hardware and software designed by *other* hardware and software—and nobody really knows how
they work. They've gotten way too complicated.
For example, you might ask a supercomputer for
the secret of life, the universe, and everything, and
after a few months of light-speed processing you
might get an answer like . . .

$$\sqrt{1.96} \times (30 \div 10^0)$$

. . . and you would have no idea what that
means.

But there is no way any mere human could

follow that logic all the way back to its binary origins. There are things that happen during the computing process that not even Gilbert Bates himself could understand. And every so often a computer will generate a piece of information that makes no sense whatsoever.

But to the machines it is all perfectly binary. 101010. On/off. Yes/no. Black/white. They are utterly, maddeningly logical.

Computers do not make mistakes.

So when you ask a computer "What is two plus two?" and the computer tells you the answer is five, you can count on two things being true: 1) There is no way, and 2) Why.

A few years ago a Crawdad Super 3785 owned by the FBI predicted that a small group of Jamaican terrorists would kidnap a US ambassador during a gamers convention in Baraboo, Wisconsin. No one believed the computer's warning. For one thing, so far as anyone at the FBI knew, there was no such thing as a Jamaican terrorist. And no ambassador was supposed to be anywhere *near* Baraboo. The warning was ignored . . . until a group calling itself the Jamaican Yahmon Liberation Army snatched a US ambassador.

At a gamers convention.

In Baraboo.

The FBI was all over Crawdad Computing,

demanding to know how their computer had predicted the event. Crawdad's response? *We don't know.*

Here in Flinkwater we call that the WDK Factor or, in severe cases, the WD*F*K Factor, which stands for We Don't *Flinking* Know. More or less.

13

Corpus Callosum

"I embedded some images of J.G. in the Brazen Bull animation," Billy said.

"I know. I saw them," I said.

"You did?"

"Yeah. So did Barney."

He gave me an uncomprehending look. "Who's Barney?"

"My cat! He totally spazzed."

"Oh. Um . . . so you didn't bonk?"

"Do I look bonked to you? Don't answer that. I took precautions."

"Interesting that not everybody bonks," Billy said.

"Wait—are you saying that you were intentionally putting people in a coma?"

"No! I just wanted to make people hate J.G."

"Everybody already hates J.G.," I said.

"I thought by putting those images in everybody's head I could kick it up a notch. I didn't expect the . . . er . . . side effects. Like I said, it's got to be the WDK Factor. Something in the way the system executed my commands caused a feedback loop in the corpus callosum. At least, that's one theory."

The corpus callosum, in case you don't know, is a thick, fibrous band of nerve tissue that connects the left brain to the right brain. It works sort of like the northbridge chip in an antique PC, shunting information back and forth between the brain halves, so that the right brain (the feeling and visualizing half) and the left brain (the logic and language half) can operate in sync. If the corpus callosum is damaged, you get a person who can only read with one eye and only cry with the other.

At least that's how my biology teacher explained it. I'm sure it's way more complicated than that, but I'm trying to get to the part that you actually want to know about, which is *How come all the bonking?*

"I think it has to do with cognitive dissonance," Billy was saying. "That's when you have two incompatible things going on in your head at the same time."

"I *know* what cognitive dissonance is," I said. I didn't really, but I didn't want Billy to think I was stupid.

"Anyway," he continued, "those images of J.G. must have caused a feedback loop in the corpus callosum. I have an idea how we can fix it."

"With the Projac?"

"Yeah. You ever hear of electroconvulsive therapy?"

"Wasn't that a twentieth-century torture technique?"

"Actually, it's still used to treat depression and a bunch of other stuff. Basically, you run a current through somebody's brain to reboot them."

"How do you know about stuff like that?"

"I was reading about ways to make my brother less of a jerk."

"And now what? Are you planning to walk into the hospital and start blasting people with the Projac?"

He grinned. "We'll start with J.G."

"Why J.G.? He's the last person I'd want to wake up."

"True. But this is an experimental treatment. If the shock turns him from a vegetable into a fungus . . . I'd just as soon it be J.G. and not somebody else."

"Brotherly love," I muttered.

"Have you ever had your nostrils glued together?"

I'd thought the hospital was crowded last night, but that was nothing compared to this. Now there were unconscious people on gurneys lined up along the hallways, laid out on the carpet in the lobby, and propped up on chairs in the waiting room. It took us twenty minutes to find J.G. He was stashed in a second-floor room with four other vegetating victims. A tired-looking nurse was checking on them. We stood politely by and waited for her to leave.

Johnston George was a nice-looking kid when he was comatose. You might mistake him for the sort of boy who would walk an elderly woman across the street or help a kitten down out of a tree—even though he would be more likely to trip the old lady and set fire to the cat.

As soon as the nurse left the room, Billy pulled the Projac out of his pocket and pointed it at J.G.'s head.

"Wait!" I said. "Are you sure this is going to work?"

"Nope," said Billy.

He pulled the trigger.

14

Awakenings

The flash of a Projac is not as bright and colorful as the ray guns you see in science fiction movies. It was more like the beam of a dim flashlight in a dusty room. Its sound was wimpy too—sort of like the *ghaaak* sound Barney makes when he barfs up a hairball. But the gun's effect on J.G. was dramatic. His body elevated itself off the bed as if the mattress had exploded.

J.G. bounced off the mattress and sat up, looking around wildly. He did not look so nice anymore. His eyes landed on Billy.

"You little *turd*!" J.G. croaked. "I'm gonna—"

Billy pulled the trigger again. In fact, he pulled it three more times, sending J.G. into all manner of airborne convulsions. When he flopped down on the bed for the final time, J.G.'s eyes were pointing in two different directions and his tongue was hanging out—but at least he was unbonked.

"It worked," said Billy, gazing with wonder at the Projac.

J.G. was beginning to move again. "Maybe we should go," I said.

"Right. But first . . ." Billy took aim at one of the other bonked patients—it happened to be Theo Winkleman, the very first SCIC victim—and zapped him. Theo convulsed, his eyes popped open, and he sat up, looking around confusedly.

I said, "Billy! You can't just randomly shoot people!"

"You *shot* me?" Theo said.

Billy aimed the Projac at the next patient.

I grabbed his arm. "Wait! We don't know how much power that thing has left. We have to make sure we wake up the right people first."

J.G.'s eyes were coming back into focus. He was trying to sit up.

"Time to go," I said.

We found my dad on the third floor. He had his own private room. My mom was sleeping in a side chair next to his bed. She looked half-bonked herself.

"Do you want to do it, or should I?" Billy whispered.

"Better let me," I said. "He's my dad." I took the

Projac and aimed it. "Do I shoot at his head, or anywhere?"

"I don't think it matters," Billy said.

It felt too weird to point the gun at my dad's head, so I shot him in the chest.

It worked instantly. His eyes opened and he sat up, putting his hands to his head to make sure it was still attached. My mom, awakened by the *ghaaak* of the Projac, had a similarly bewildered expression.

"Dad? Are you okay?" I asked.

"What happened?" he asked.

"You bonked," I said.

He noticed the Projac in my hand and his eyes widened.

As I have mentioned, the Projac was a top secret weapons project, and the fact that it was being wielded by his very own daughter was almost enough to send him straight back into his coma.

But before he could say anything, four men charged into the room waving guns, shouting at us to *flinking* get our gosh darn derrieres on the *flinking* floor. Except that wasn't *exactly* what they said.

I immediately dove for the floor, but Billy just stood there with his mouth hanging open, staring in admiration and disbelief at the display of raw testosterone and SWAT team weaponry.

Luckily, they didn't shoot him.

15

The Most Popular Kid in Flinkwater

You'd think we would be hailed as heroes for saving the people of Flinkwater from SCIC, but that wasn't what happened. Instead of getting our pictures taken while receiving the key to the city and a big fat reward check, Billy and I got our pictures taken at the police station, holding nine-digit numbers under our chins.

The charges? Stealing an illegal weapon. Possessing an illegal weapon. Firing an illegal weapon. Assault with an illegal weapon.

Fortunately, the Projac was *so* illegal and *so* top secret that ACPOD security—aka my dad—whisked us out of the police station a few hours after we were arrested and managed to get the whole affair hushed up.

Sort of.

Because even after Billy and I cured SCIC and all the hospitalized people went home and the Brazen Bull was deleted from every tablet, desktop, and phone in Flinkwater, the DHS remained. You could hardly walk down the street without seeing a few black, tinted-windowed SUVs patrolling the streets.

As soon as they gave us our phones back, I called Uncle Ashton.

"Ginger, baby, I've been worrying about you! Are y'all still bubbled?"

"Not so much," I said. I told him about me and Billy and the Projac. "The fence is mostly still there, but they've opened the roads in and out of town. The airport is open. And we got our tabs back."

"That's a heck of a tale," he said. "How's your momma?"

"She's still a little cranky."

He laughed—a torture test for the little speaker in my phone.

"Ginger, baby, your mama knows more about cranky than a pit full of rattlesnakes. Is the DHS is still hanging around?"

"Yeah. But I don't know why."

"They're gonna be hard to get rid of, punkin. How's your hacker boyfriend doing?"

"He's not my boyfriend," I said, thinking, *Not yet, anyway*.

Uncle Ashton chuckled.

"Besides," I said, "Billy didn't do it on purpose."

"Not saying he did. But maybe there's more than one gator in that hole. When a primary government contractor like ACPOD gets hacked, the DHS ain't gonna believe it was just because some kid got bullied by his brother. Not sure I believe it either. Something don't smell right. That Brazen Bull, punkin, might be jest a cud-chewing heifer straddlin' a rattler den."

Uncle Ashton can be overly fond of animal metaphors. And, as I've mentioned, he's kind of paranoid. I'm *sure* he used to be a spy.

"Are you saying the DHS is going to stay in Flinkwater?" I said.

"Baby, they're like ticks on a hound."

As for J.G., Billy's revenge backfired. Everybody who had viewed the subliminalized Brazen Bull became weirdly fascinated by J.G. Even though they had no *conscious* memory of it, his face was embedded in their *sub*conscious. Girls were literally *throwing* themselves at him, and guys who had always avoided contact with J.G. for fear of wedgies or worse suddenly wanted to be his friend.

Stunned and flattered by all the attention, J.G. forgot that he was a psychotic monster and started acting like a regular person.

Billy had a theory, of course.

"They don't consciously remember what they saw on the screen. All they know is that J.G. is somehow special, and they want to be special too."

"Some revenge. You've made him the most popular kid in Flinkwater."

"At least he's not gluing people's nostrils together."

That was true. Billy's attempt to avenge himself on his brother had accidentally-on-purpose made the world a better place.

But not for long. I'd like to say that we went back to what normally passes for normal in Flinkwater, but I'd be lying. Uncle Ashton was right. Compared to what happened next, the Brazen Bull was nothing but a cud-chewing heifer. Standing over a rattlesnake den.

Episode Two

The Digital Dog

16

Grounded

I forgot to mention that as a reward for saving the people of Flinkwater from the plague of bonking, I got punished.

After my dad got me and Billy released from the police station, I figured everything was going to be okay. Dad was just happy to be conscious again, and to have George G. George off his case.

"Dealing with George is exhausting," he said. "All the man knows how to do is scowl and shout, and he never stops."

"Do you ever yell back at him?" I asked.

"I don't think yelling would work. I just grit my teeth and picture him wearing pink polka-dot boxer shorts. It helps." He smiled. "But it's hard not to laugh."

I laughed.

Things didn't go so good with Mom. The first

thing she said to me when we got home was, "You're grounded."

It was so unfair I was rendered speechless.

"And no Internet," she added. "One week."

"A *week*?" I said. "What am I supposed to do? Watch the DustBots clean?"

"And maybe do some cleaning yourself," she said.

I looked to Dad for help and saw him shaking his head at me, as in, *Do Not Go There*. Clearly, I was not about to argue my way out of this one.

To make sure I didn't try to get online while she was at work, Mom disabled our home net access and took my cell.

It was like being bonked, but without the advantage of being unconscious.

That week could have been the most tedious seven days of my life. I say "could have been" only because Billy had given me a special router and the codes to his Poopnet. I could access the nets on my tab, as long as I was within six feet of some plumbing.

I got through the first few days by sitting in the bathroom playing Ghast Wars. I wasn't that into gaming, but Billy was, so I spent hours as the Witch Queen Baldaba, attempting to entice Billy's Stranglan Warrior into my posh, extremely palatial dungeon. The virtual experience was marred, unfortunately, by my constant awareness that the images I was receiving were being transmitted through sixteen miles of sewer pipe. Also, I had to keep one ear open to listen for my mother. One hint that I had managed to get online and she'd unplug every device I owned, add another week to my sentence, and make me perform some heinous domestic task better left to the DustBots.

So there I was, a virtual witch queen imprisoned by a Real World witch queen, condemned to long days of incarceration and capital-*B* Boredom. I might have gone completely insane, if not for Redge, the talking dog.

17

Redge

Talking dogs are nothing new. Dogs have been talking since that first wolf cub was stolen from its den by some Cro-Magnon who didn't happen to be hungry enough at the moment to eat it. Problem was, for the first fifty thousand years or so, dogs couldn't speak English. They spoke *dog*.

Redge changed all that.

I had been sitting, morosely watching the digital clock on my computer tick off the seconds of my sentence while waiting for Billy to come back online—he had excused himself to go do something Real World, like eat or pee—when I heard my witch queen mother shouting. It sounded like she was yelling, "Go away! Go away, you nasty thing!"

I ran out of my room to find out what sort of nasty thing she was yelling at, and found her standing in the front door staring down at an exceedingly sad and droopy-looking basset hound. I looked from my mother to the dog, then back to my mother, then back to the dog.

My mother has a thing about dogs. She tolerates my cat, but she really, *really* does not like dogs. A barking dog would make her quiver with rage; a growling dog would make her growl back; a whining dog would set her teeth on edge. But I could not imagine what she was feeling at that moment, because this dog was doing something completely different.

This dog was talking.

"*. . are you afraid? Please don't be afraid. I'm sorry. My name is Redge. May I have a treat? Your perfume is unpleasant, but I like the smell of your feet. I'm sorry. A treat would be very nice. I will lick you if you give me a treat. Do you want me to lick you first?*"

"Shut up, you stupid dog!" she said.

The dog looked up and blinked his basset hound eyes. "*Shut up? Okay. I will shut up. I will shut up right now. See? I am a good dog. I—*"

"Stop talking!" she said.

The dog threw his head back and bayed mournfully. The howl of a basset hound is a sound to send chills up and down your spine. You would think it impossible to howl and talk at the same time, but even as the beast's bellow filled the air, it kept on talking.

"I'm sorry! I'm sorry!"

The words coming from the dog were not actually coming out of his mouth. They were coming from a tiny speaker attached to his collar. I realized then that the dog wasn't really *talking*. Instead, the dog's *thoughts* were being voiced by some technological device.

"I would like to be friends. Friends give friends treats. I am Redge." I felt around his collar until I found a switch. *"I am a good dog—"*

Click.

The talking stopped. The dog immediately perked up and began wagging his tail. I turned back to my mom.

"That does it," she said, backing into the house.

"What are you going to do?" I asked.

"Call Animal Control," she said.

18

The Collar

"Wait!" I said, thinking fast. "I know whose dog he is. Why don't I just walk him home?"

It was a long shot. Technically, I was still grounded. And I had no idea where this talking dog had come from. But the very last thing I wanted was for this sad-looking hound to be turned over to Animal Control, the equivalent of death row for dogs.

My mother was still in a somewhat addled state. The tips of her spiky hair were sagging, and all she really wanted was a closed and locked door between her and this dog.

"You're grounded," she said.

"I'll come straight home."

I could see her crumbling—a rare occurrence where my mother was concerned—but the sooner Redge was out of her life, the better.

"Well . . . all right, then. See that you do."

I looked at the dog. The dog looked at me. Have you ever looked into a basset hound's eyes? They are enormous brown pools of *I Love You*. I know those eyes evolved over thousands of generations of manipulating humans to provide food and shelter—but I was helpless before their beseeching power. The dog *loved* me! Redge *needed* me! He was insanely grateful that I had silenced the yammering speaker attached to his collar. I had to *save* him!

My first instinct was to remove the collar, but when I tried to do so, I found that the collar was no ordinary collar. Two thin wires ran from the collar into the back of his skull.

That pretty much confirmed what I already suspected. The talking dog was another demented product developed by the engineers at ACPOD.

I do not *literally* mean that the engineers at ACPOD are demented, although several of them might fit that description. What I *mean* is, the engineers whose job it is to develop new products for ACPOD exist in a sort of virtual reality in which ideas are more important than, say, people. Or dogs. Like the men and women who invented the machine gun, the atomic bomb, and high heels, they don't concern themselves with Real World consequences.

Billy George, for example, might grow up one

day to become an ACPOD engineer. That does not make him a bad person. Billy is a sweetheart. But if he conceived of a way to make someone's brain explode, he might become so excited by the technology of it that he would forget about the brain in question belonging to some Real World individual. Like you. Or me.

I could just imagine some of the conversations leading up to the dog collar: "You know what would be cool? If dogs could talk! Let's drill some holes in a dog's skull and see what happens!"

Yeah, right. One look at poor Redge and any normal person would know that nobody—not even a basset hound—wants everybody to know what they're thinking.

As I was having these private thoughts, Redge was sniffing around the patch of neglected grass that doubles as our front yard. Naturally, he found something stinky to roll in—possibly a dead worm, or worse.

"Stupid dog," I said.

Redge hopped to his stumpy legs and waddled over to share his new cologne with me.

"No thank you, stupid dog," I said.

He barked. His bark sounded exactly like his name: Redge.

"Okay, _Redge_. Please do not share your stinky

discovery with me, Redge. Thank you."

He seemed to understand. Anyway, he stopped, sat back on his haunches and produced a questioning whine.

"Come, Redge," I said. "I want you to meet a friend of mine."

19

Mrs. Duchakis

I tied the belt from my dad's terry-cloth bathrobe to Redge's collar and we set off for the Duchakises'. Because when you think "dog," you think "animal," and when you think "animal," you think Myke Duchakis. Myke was the president and founder of Flinkwater High's AAPT Club. AAPT stands for Animals Are People Too.

Seven years ago, on his sixth birthday, Myke's parents had taken him to the 4-H barn at the Iowa State Fair, where he met a piglet named Bacon. Young Mykey's favorite food—up until that moment—had been bacon.

"Daddy, why did they name him Bacon?" Mykey asked.

His daddy, an ACPOD engineer with the people skills of a rabid hyena, explained in graphic detail the facts of farm life and slaughterhouse death. They'd had to carry Myke out of the 4-H barn, screaming his lungs out.

At that moment, Myke Duchakis became a vegetarian, and a champion of all creatures great and small.

Myke lived on Gilbert Avenue—normally a ten-minute walk, but with Redge having to sniff every lamppost and fire hydrant, and pee on most of them, it took us half an hour to get there. I counted seven black SUVs cruising the streets.

Uncle Ashton was right—the DHS was on Flinkwater like ticks on a dog.

My plan—I always have a plan, in case you haven't noticed—was to introduce Redge to Myke, have them instantly bond, then leave the dog in his care. It was a good plan, but like many good plans, it was not without flaws, the first one being that the door was answered by Mrs. Duchakis, a round-headed, round-bodied woman with graying hair that she wore long and straight in a failed attempt to make her face look thinner.

"Is Myke home?" I asked, giving her my best smile.

"Oh Dear Lord," she said, looking at Redge.

Unsure how to respond to that, I waited for more.

"Dear God in Heaven," she added unhelpfully.

I tried turning up my smile a notch.

"Lord Save Us," she said.

All this talk of the Lord was making both Redge and me uneasy. I had not factored the Almighty into my plan.

"I hope to heaven that is *your* dog, Ms. Crump," she said, "and not some stray creature you are hoping to foist upon our overpopulated household."

What can I say? The woman was a mind reader.

"I just wanted to introduce him to Myke," I said.

Mrs. Duchakis sighed, and when she sighed, her head sank so low between her shoulders that it looked as if it was about to disappear turtlelike into her ample torso.

"He's back in his menagerie," she said.

20

Myke

It may be that the reason Myke Duchakis had so many animals was that he himself was adopted. From his name you might expect Mycroft Duchakis to be a half-British-half-Greek aristocrat. Myke wasn't like that at all. He claimed his biological parents were from Egypt. Physically he had the look of a North African desert prince raised on French fries and Iowa sweet corn. In other words, he was as round as his adoptive mother.

Redge and I found Myke in his bedroom—aka the menagerie—feeding cheese curls to a three-legged squirrel. It was a peaceful scene—a boy and his squirrel—until the squirrel got an eyeful of Redge, and Redge spotted the squirrel. Naturally, the squirrel being a squirrel, and Redge being a dog, things got very exciting.

Again, not part of my plan.

Redge let out a soul-shattering bellow, sending the squirrel rocketing toward the ceiling. I had not known that squirrels could cling to ceilings, but apparently they can, even three-legged ones. Myke also attempted to levitate himself, but he was not so successful. The other various creatures in the room—one chinchilla, several mice, a pigeon, a guinea pig, and a leopard gecko—began running, flapping, squeaking, squawking, and hissing frantically. Fortunately, all but the squirrel were in cages. I grabbed Redge by the collar and dragged him out of the room while Myke ran from cage to cage, frantically attempting to calm himself and his tenants. I shut the door and waited in the hall.

Myke was a little upset with me. I couldn't blame him. I should have known his bedroom would be full of small creatures he had rescued over the years, and I knew Redge was, well, a *dog*. I just hadn't put together that those two things didn't mix well. As my dad would say, I had not *synthesized* all available data. Oh well.

After a few minutes, Myke poked his head out and suggested—rather stiffly, I thought—that we retire to the backyard.

"Sammy could have hurt himself!" Myke said, by way of initiating our conversation. We were sitting outside by his rabbit hutch. I had tied Redge to the leg of my lawn chair. He was looking longingly at the two flop-eared bunnies who were peering nervously out from their chicken-wire enclosure.

"Who's Sammy?" I asked.

Myke rolled his eyes. "My *squirrel*?"

"Oh. Sorry about that."

"They're innocent creatures, you know!"

I could tell that Myke was about to go on one of his Animals Are People Too rants, so I hit the switch on Redge's collar.

"*—never seen one of those before! They look like squirrels. Fat squirrels with long ears! I am a good dog. I—*"

"Shut up, Redge," Myke said.

"*—would like to play with those squirrels and maybe eat one too. My name is—*"

Myke reached over and switched off the collar.

I think my mouth was hanging open.

"You two know each other?" I said.

"Of course," he said. "I busted him out of jail just last week."

21

The Uncanny Valley

"A couple of weeks ago, before all that SCIC stuff happened, my dad said he wanted to show me something cool," Myke said, making a face. "You know how my dad is—he's always showing me stuff he thinks will make me more manly."

I nodded. Myke's dad moonlighted as the Brazen Bulls' football coach.

"So I went over to where he was working— you know that long gray building way in the back of the ACPOD campus?"

"Area Fifty-One," I said. We called it that because the building in question had extra security, and nobody outside of the engineers who worked there knew what went on inside.

"Yeah, well, that's where my dad works," Myke said. "Turns out they do cybernetics experiments on animals there. My dad arranged a special pass for me and introduced me to Redge. He thought I'd think it was cool to talk to a dog."

I looked at Redge, who was now lying on his belly, his long snout pointed at the rabbit hutch. "Does he understand what we're saying?"

"No more than any other dog," Myke said.

"I don't get it. ACPOD makes robots. Why are they doing animal experiments?"

"To my dad, animals are just flesh-and-blood robots," Myke said. "I think they're trying to make them more robotic."

"By making them talk? That's sort of creepy."

"I know," Myke said, looking at Redge. "It's like the Uncanny Valley."

I remember my first visit to the Uncanny Valley like it was yesterday. I was four years old, and my dad brought home one of the very first Dustbunnies. Remember Dustbunny?

The D-Monix Dustbunny was the first self-actuating quasi-intelligent cleaning bot for the home. According to D-Monix CEO Josh Stevens, it was the invention that would "change everything."

"No more wiping, sweeping, polishing, scrubbing, or dusting," he said in the video ads. "Just sit back and let Dustbunny do the work!"

My mom hates cleaning, so she bought one the first day it went on sale. She took it out of the box, put it on the living room floor, and turned it on. I thought it was a real rabbit. It looked like one, right down to the floppy ears and the blinking black eyes. But when I tried to pet it, it was cold and plasticky-feeling. I screamed.

Don't get me wrong; I love robots. But when a robot starts looking like something that is alive, it's sort of disturbing. That creepy feeling is called the Uncanny Valley.

The Uncanny Valley isn't an actual valley, it's more like a feeling. It was named back in the last century, when robotics researchers realized that making robots that looked and acted like people was not such a good idea. A metal humanoid robot like C3PO from the old Star Wars movies was fine. Who doesn't love C3PO? But when humanoid robots got realistic skin and eyes and smiles, people didn't love them so much. It's just too . . . *uncanny*. Robots should look like robots, not people. Or bunnies.

Mom thought the Dustbunny was creepy too, so she returned it. So did a lot of other people. A few months later ACPOD introduced the smaller, quieter, distinctly robotic DustBot. It was a huge success. We have six of them. The DustBot was the product that made Gilbert Bates a billionaire, while the failure of Dustbunny nearly bankrupted D-Monix Industries.

Josh Stevens went ballistic. He claimed that Gilbert Bates had stolen his idea. The battle in court lasted for years. In the end ACPOD won the case. Ever since then D-Monix has stayed out of the robot business and focused on computers. Dustbunny was Josh Stevens's greatest failure.

But I gotta say, his D-Monix computers rock.

"My dad says that eventually they'll be able to program animals like computers. He's working with D-Monix Industries to develop a set of controls that wire right into an animal's brain."

"D-Monix? Why? They're ACPOD's biggest competitor!"

"D-Monix developed the hardware interface and licensed it to ACPOD last year. George G. George himself is overseeing the project. Anyway, I didn't think it was cool at all, sticking wires in a dog's head. I could tell right away that poor Redge was freaking out, having that voice come out of his collar. I sort of freaked out myself—I mean, it really is Uncanny Valley territory, hearing that dog talk."

"Yeah, you should've seen my mom. She's scared of nothing, but hearing Redge talk just about curled her hair."

"Your mom doesn't have curly hair."

"Exactly. So what did you do when your dad introduced you to Redge?"

"I started yelling," Myke said. "Telling my dad he had to let the animals go. Redge wasn't the only one—they had some monkeys wired up too, only they weren't talking. Except for one who kept yelling something about 'stinky no-tails.' I think Redge here was their first success story. If you call that success. Of course they didn't listen to me, and my dad hustled me out of there. So I went back a few days later and busted him out."

"You just walked into ACPOD's most secure building and walked out with a dog?"

"When I was there with my dad, I sort of broke the lock on the south door, at the back of the building. It looks like it's locked, but if you jiggle the handle from the outside, it pops right open."

"I still can't believe you didn't get caught. Doesn't that building have all kinds of extra security?"

"This was a few days ago. Practically everybody was bonked, remember? And the only guard on duty was an AAPT member."

"AAPT has members?" I had thought Myke was the only one.

"*Many* members," he said, daring me to doubt him.

"Wow. I had no idea, So, the guard just ignored you?"

"I told him I wanted to visit Redge. He put the security cameras on an infinite loop and disabled the infrared sensors."

"So you just walked in and let Redge out?"

"That's right. I was going to let all the animals go. I got one of the monkey cages open, but that didn't work out so good."

I looked at Redge. "Let me guess. . . ."

"You don't have to guess. Redge took off after the monkey. The last I saw of him, they were tearing down the hallway. That monkey could move! The guard and I looked for an hour. We finally gave up and I came home." He shrugged. "I figured they were still in the building, but obviously they got out. At least Redge did."

"What happened to the monkey?"

Myke shrugged, regarding the dog with something less than love. "What are you going to do with him?"

"Me? *You're* the one who let him out!"

"Yeah, but I can't keep him. As soon as my dad sees him, it's back to the lab."

"Well *I* can't keep him! For one thing, my mom is one hundred percent anti-dog. Also, Barney would kill him."

"Barney your cat? He's only a quarter Redge's size," Myke pointed out.

"Yeah, but he's tough. Our DustBots are terrified of him."

Redge had waddled off a few paces and found something new to roll in. He must have triggered the switch on his collar, because the next thing we heard was, *"—itchy-itchy-itchy. I am a good dog. My name is Redge. Autopsy Monday. Monday autopsy for Redge. Dr. Ostley says good dog Redge. . . ."*

Myke and I looked at each other.

"Monday is autopsy day, Dr. Ostley, dog food, treat, dog food . . ."

"Do you think he knows what he's saying?" I asked.

". . . crunchy dog food. Smelling good dog food. . . ."

"I think he knows what he *heard,*" said Myke. "I think he heard this Dr. Ostley say something about doing an autopsy on Monday."

"Autopsy, as in you have to be dead to have one, right?"

"Redge is hungry. Redge would like his dog food now . . ."

"Yeah." Mike walked over to Redge, patted his head—

". . . yum-yum dog food—"

—and switched off the collar.

"Monday is tomorrow," Myke said. "If they find him, he's dead! We have to do something."

I was staring hard at Redge. "You know, except for that collar, he looks like any other basset hound," I said.

"So?"

"So what we do is we figure out how to get that collar off him."

Taking off an ordinary dog collar is easy, but what do you do when the collar is hardwired into a dog's brain?

Myke examined the two leads attached to Redge's skull. "I'm afraid if we just yank the wires out we'll kill him."

"How about if we cut the wires?"

"I don't know. . . ."

"We need technical advice," I said.

22

Plan A

My future husband, Billy George, lived in the old part of town—not far from Addy Gumm, but in a much nicer, much bigger house. In fact, he lived in the grandest house in town, a fortresslike three-story brick edifice built in the middle of the last century by a paranoid corn baron named Wilhelm Krause.

If anybody could figure out how to get that collar off, it would be Billy. I asked Myke if I could use his bathroom and, to keep our communication secure, contacted Billy over the Poopnet. Billy told me to bring Redge to the corner of Bates Avenue and Twelfth Street.

Myke and I set off with Redge in tow, keeping a sharp eye out for black SUVs. We made it to Bates and Twelfth without incident, but Billy was nowhere to be seen.

"Are you sure we have the right place?" Myke asked.

Redge started barking furiously.

"Shut up, Redge," I said.

"Look!" said Myke.

I looked. At first I didn't understand what I was seeing. A black stick, or wand, or feeler—or *something*— was poking out of the hole at the center of a manhole cover. It had a small crook at the end. As I watched, the wand slowly rotated.

Redge wanted to eat it. Or at least bite it. Myke, with both hands on the leash, struggled to hold him back.

The thing finally fixed upon us and remained still. I saw the glint of a lens and deduced that we were being observed by a fiber-optic periscope. I waved, hoping it was Billy.

The periscope withdrew into the sewer. A moment later the edge of the manhole cover tipped up. A hand appeared and slid the cover aside. Billy's head popped out.

Redge wagged his tail uncertainly.

"Come on!" Billy said. "Hurry, before somebody sees you." He lowered himself back into the sewer.

I peered down into the hole. Billy was climbing down a series of steel rungs into the darkness.

"Are you sure?" I said doubtfully.

"Yes!" His voice echoed up from below.

Redge came up beside me, looked down the hole, growled, and backed away.

"I think that means no," Myke said. "Dogs aren't good with ladders."

I stuck my head down the hole and yelled, "Hey, Billy!" I could see his flashlight bobbing around twenty feet below.

"Come on!" he yelled back.

"The dog won't go! We need to go to plan B!"

A few seconds later the light was shining straight up at me.

"What's plan B?" he asked.

"You don't have a plan B?"

He didn't say anything for a few seconds.

Then he said, "Give me a minute."

"Hurry up! I'm in the middle of the street with my head down a manhole!"

"Okay! Here's what we do. . . ."

23

Plan B

Plan B wasn't much better than plan A. According to Billy, there was a large culvert underneath Highway 18 where it crossed the Raccoona River. The opening was covered with a steel grate, but Billy said he could open it.

"How?" I asked.

"You'll see," Billy said. "You guys take the dog over to Flinkwater Park and down to the bike trail along the river. Follow the trail up to the overpass. I'll take the sewer route and meet you there. . . . What's wrong?"

"What about the *Sasquatch*?" Myke said.

I laughed.

Myke glared at me.

Maybe you've never heard of the Flinkwater Sasquatch. Ever since I was a kid, there have

been stories about a wild, shaggy, manlike creature haunting the park. Flinkwater Park is not
your ordinary park—it's a state park, more than six
miles long, covering three thousand acres of steep,
wooded coulees and bottomland on the north side
of the Raccoona River. Every now and then, some
terrified hiker reports seeing a big hairy humanoid creature. A few wildlife enthusiasts have set up
heat-sensing cameras in the woods, but all they've
caught on film have been coyotes, deer, raccoons,
and bobcats. Most intelligent people don't take the
Sasquatch thing seriously.

Myke, however, did.

"The Flinkwater Sasquatch is an urban myth," I
said.

"It's not! Lots of people have seen it."

"Like who?"

"Like Billy's brother," Myke said, looking down
into the sewer.

"J.G. makes stuff up to scare people," Billy said.

"Addy Gumm saw it once."

"She's just a crazy old lady," Billy said from
the sewer.

"She is not! Besides, even the police were out
looking for it."

I said, "Myke, they got a report from some pic-
nickers and searched every inch of the park. No

Sasquatch. It was just some people who got freaked out by a big dog or something. Besides, we'll have Redge with us. He eats Sasquatch for breakfast."

Myke wasn't convinced, but if I was willing to risk a Sasquatch event, he had to go along with it.

I was startled by the blast of a car horn. I had forgotten that I was kneeling in the middle of the street looking into a storm sewer.

"What was *that*?" Billy asked.

"We gotta go." I jumped up and waved to Gerald Ruff, who was pounding impatiently on the horn of his pickup truck. I pointed at the open manhole. Gerald Ruff got out of his truck.

"What in the tarnation of hailstorm are you kids doing playing in the middle of the ding-dang street?" Gerald Ruff was the owner of Ruff Roofs, a roofing contractor headquartered in nearby Halibut. I knew him because he'd replaced the shingles on our house the previous summer.

"*Ruff! Roof!*" said Redge. I thought for a second that his collar had been activated—but it was just him barking.

"That's one smart dog you got there," said Gerald Ruff.

"We saw this manhole cover was off," I said quickly. "I was trying to get it back over the hole."

"I can help with that," he said. In a few seconds he had dragged the cover back in place. "There ya go."

"Thanks, Mr. Ruff," I said.

"Ruff!" said Redge.

Gerald Ruff said, "That old hound would make a great mascot for my business."

"Yeah . . . um . . . we have to get going," I said. "See you later."

24

Sasquatch

We followed the main trail through the park down to the bike path. Myke kept an eye out for Sasquatch, while Redge ranged back and forth at the end of his terry-cloth leash, sniffing everything. We reached the bike path without incident and followed it along the river to the Highway 18 overpass. Billy was waiting inside the six-foot-tall culvert, looking through the heavy steel grate, wearing a pair of welder's goggles and holding a device that looked like a cross between a power drill and a machine gun.

"Better stand back," he said.

We backed off a few feet.

"Way back," he said.

The bars that were supposed to keep people out of the storm sewers looked formidable, but they were no match for the thing in Billy's hands.

He pulled the trigger, and an intensely bright beam
of greenish-blue light shot out, melting the steel bars
like a hot knife cutting through butter, sending out
a spatter of bright orange globules of molten steel.

It took him about thirty seconds to completely
destroy the grate. The ends of the bars glowed
orange. Curls of smoke rose up from the ground
where the spatters had landed. Billy stepped out of
the culvert, placing his feet carefully so as not to
get a hotfoot. He pushed the goggles up onto his
forehead and grinned at us.

Blinking away afterimages, I said, "What was
that?"

"Acetylene laser," Billy said—as if a handheld
acetylene laser was a perfectly normal accessory
for a thirteen-year-old to be carrying around.

Myke said, "Where . . . how . . ."

Billy said, "I made it."

Have I mentioned that Billy George is a mad
genius?

"I thought it might come in handy some day,"
Billy said.

"Hey, guys . . . ," Myke said.

I ignored him, looking into the dark and
exceedingly spooky sewer.

"Um . . . I'm not sure Redge wants to go in
there," I said.

"Guys . . ."

"Redge will go anyplace we do," Billy said. "You're the one that's scared."

"I'm not scared," I said. But I was.

"Guys!"

I turned to see Myke pointing a shaking finger at something in the woods. At first I couldn't see what he was pointing at.

And then I did. It looked like a man—an extremely tall man—with a body made out of leaves and the head of a Rastafarian Wookiee, standing not thirty feet from us in the shadow of a cedar grove.

"Sasquatch!" I screamed. I grabbed Redge and dove through the sewer grate into the culvert. Myke was right behind me.

Billy said, "Hey!" Then he saw what we had seen, and he was running too. We turned left, then right, then left again, and didn't stop until we were all gasping for breath.

"I . . . think . . . we . . . lost him," Billy said.

We listened for the sound of Sasquatch footsteps.

Dead silence.

"Maybe Sasquatches don't like sewers," Myke said hopefully.

"*Nobody* likes sewers," I said.

I heard a whispery, scurrying sound.

"What's *that*?"

"Nothing," Billy said. "Just some rats."

25

In the Sewers

The inside of a storm sewer is not as gross as you might think. All the really nasty stuff goes in a different system of pipes and ends up in the treatment plant. The storm sewer just carries runoff from the streets, and it hadn't rained lately, so except for a few puddly sections, we didn't have to do any wading. But that doesn't mean it was pleasant. Our walk through the culverts and passageways took us past two extremely stinky, extremely dead raccoons, and way too many sets of beady rat eyes. I didn't know Flinkwater *had* rats. We could hear them scurrying ahead of us.

One good thing: With all those rats to think about I forgot to worry about the Sasquatch.

Redge did not care for the sewer at all. He whined and growled and snarled and moaned—sometimes all at once. To my relief, he did not mistake the rats for squirrels. He just wanted to get out of there.

So did I. The time we spent making our way through those wet, echoey passageways supplied me with nightmare material for the rest of my life—not that I needed it after our Sasquatch encounter.

"Do you know where we are?" I asked Billy as we hit another intersection.

"Uh . . . yeah, pretty much."

"Pretty much?"

"I think we go right."

We turned right and heard a massive amount of scurrying ahead of us.

"Actually, I think left would be better," he said.

I was ready to strangle him and leave him for the rats, especially after I slipped and fell headlong in a gloopy puddle of I-don't-want-to-know-what. Fortunately for him, we soon reached our destination: a concealed doorway set into the side of the sewer wall. Billy pulled a hidden lever out from a recess in the wall, and the door swung open to reveal a narrow staircase leading up. We climbed the stairs to another door and found ourselves in Billy's underground sanctuary.

I have mentioned Billy's underground bunker before, but allow me to explain a bit more. Wilhelm Krause, the eccentric corn baron who, back in the 1950s, built the house where Billy and his family now lived, had constructed a bomb shelter in the subbasement. That bomb shelter was now Billy's bedroom.

"He must have built in this escape tunnel just in case," Billy explained. "I found it hidden behind this wall panel a few years ago. It comes in handy sometimes, like when I'm grounded, or when J.G. is being a jerk. Besides, it's fun exploring the sewers."

"That was not *fun*," I said. "That was *disgusting*."

"It was fun *and* disgusting," said Myke. "I didn't know there were so many animals living underground!"

"If you start keeping sewer rats for pets, I'm going to unfriend you," I told him.

Myke shrugged, smiling.

Redge was digging through a pile of Billy's dirty laundry.

Everybody seemed delighted with how things were going. Except for me.

"I have to change," I said.

"Into what?" Billy asked.

"Clean, dry clothes, dog breath! Look at me!"

"Oh." He looked at me. "How did you get so dirty?"

"Give me that laser thing," I said. I wasn't actually going to kill him, just clonk him over the head with it.

He must have seen something in my eyes because he backed quickly away. "There's clothes right there," he said, looking at the basket that had consumed all of Redge's head except for his floppy ears.

"*Clean* clothes," I said.

26

Framistats and Thingleberries

Billy found a pair of fresh jeans and a T-shirt with a picture of Albert Einstein sticking out his tongue. I had no idea what that meant—probably some boy joke—so I turned the shirt inside out and went into the bathroom to change. The jeans were a little loose. I had to roll the waistband a couple of times to get them to stay up. I came out looking anything but fashionable. Billy and Myke could not have cared less. They were examining the collar. Redge was looking somewhat nervous.

"Don't hurt him," I said.

Myke gave me a scathing look, letting me know that he, the founder and president of AAPT, would never cause an animal distress.

"Sorry," I said. "I wasn't thinking."

Billy was examining the two wires that ran

from the collar to the back of Redge's skull.

"I can detach them from the collar easy," he said. "But he'll still have these wires hanging out. I'm not sure how deep they go. . . . I mean, if they go all the way into his brain, he'll need surgery to get them out."

"But we can take off the collar?"

"Oh sure. Let me just unfasten the buckle and—"

I moved closer to get a better look, and I guess I wasn't watching where I was stepping. Redge let out a yelp and jerked away. There was a faint double pop. The dog screeched and ran to hide under Billy's bed.

Billy stared at the two wires hanging from the collar in his hands. Myke followed Redge under the bed. I just stood there trying hard not to lose it.

"It's okay!" Billy said. "He's gonna be okay!"

"Okay?" I said. "You just yanked wires out of his brain!"

"No I didn't." Billy was examining the ends of the wires. "Look, the wires just went to a couple of electrodes glued onto his skin." At the ends of the wires were two disks no bigger around than a pencil eraser.

I could hear Redge whining and Myke blubbering.

Billy said, "Come on out, you guys. Everything's okay."

It took a few minutes to coax Myke and Redge out from under the bed. Myke was hugging the dog and crying. I think Redge was more upset at being strangled by Myke than he was by having the wires ripped off. When Myke loosened his grip enough for us to get a good look at Redge's head, I could see that Billy was right. There were two tiny bald patches where the electrodes had been fastened.

"He's gonna be fine," Billy said.

"You could have killed him!" Myke said.

"Hey, I didn't do anything. He tore them loose himself. How come he jumped like that?"

I said, "It was me."

They looked at me.

"I sort of accidentally stepped on his tail."

We gave Redge a pound of hamburger from the freezer. As Redge gnawed happily on the brick of frozen meat, we discussed our next step.

"We've stolen a piece of ACPOD secret technology, and we're harboring a fugitive hound," I said. "That means Homeland Security is going to be coming after us, if they aren't already."

"How about we just return the collar," Myke said. "They don't care about the dog—they were going to kill him."

Billy was at his desk, using a tiny screwdriver to do something to the collar.

"What are you doing?" I asked.

"I just want to see if it—oops."

"Don't say 'oops,'" I said. "'Oops' is scary."

He was down on his hands and knees. "Dropped a screw. Here it is."

Myke said, "Once we get the collar back to Area Fifty-One, they'll stop looking for the dog. Right?"

"Except that they might want to plug the dog back in so he can tell them who kidnapped him," I said.

"True . . ."

"This is really cool," Billy said. He had the back off the collar and was examining its innards with his handheld digital microscope.

"Put it back together, Billy. Myke's right—we have to return the collar. We can tell them we found it on the street."

"You think they'll believe us?" Myke asked.

"We're just kids. All we have to do is act stupid."

"What about Redge?"

"Redge will have to lay low for a while."

"Where? He can't stay with me," Myke said.

"Me either—my mom would freak."

We both looked at Billy, who was plugging a slim cable from his tablet into the collar.

"Check this out," he said. His tablet lit up, displaying a complicated schematic.

"Wow," I said, with no idea what I was look-ing at.

"It's incredibly simple," Billy said. He then rattled off a long string of words that included "synthetic bionomic interruption circuit" and "dynamical ergonomic interface" and "adaptive cybernetics." None of which meant a thing to me.

"How fascinating," I said boredly.

"What's *really* fascinating is that it's no more complicated than a lawn-mower engine. I bet I could make it even simpler. The *gubble gubble* cir-cuit is redundant, and the *gobbledygook* is *fram-istating wingleberries. . . .*"

I looked at Myke to see if he was following any of it. Nope.

I said, "Billy. *Stop talking.*"

He stopped talking.

"Put the collar back together. Myke and I are going to get rid of it."

"Why?"

"What have we been talking about for the past half hour?"

"Cybernetic interfaces?"

"No. Put the collar together. And hurry up, before Homeland Security finds us here and *fram-istats* all over your *thingamabobs.*"

"Huh?"

"Just do it."

Billy had the collar back together within minutes. He handed it to me. I noticed some tiny printing on the inside: *DMI/ACPOD Prototype B-427.*

DMI. D-Monix Industries. What Myke had told me earlier was true. The talking dog was a D-Monix/ACPOD joint project.

I dropped the collar on the floor and stomped on it.

"What are you *doing*?" Billy said, horrified by the deliberate destruction of technology.

I picked up the collar and shook it. It produced a satisfactory rattle.

"I don't want them sticking this on some other poor dog," I said.

"Yeah, but—" Billy was interrupted by a *ding* from a little speaker above his bedroom door. His eyes widened. "Somebody's coming!" He yanked open the secret door. "Myke! Get Redge out of here! Quick!"

Myke snatched the remains of the frozen hamburger and ran through the door to the sewers. "Redge, come!" Myke said

"Ruff!" said Redge, and followed Myke into the sewers.

Billy slammed the door. A second later the other door opened and Billy's father stepped into the room.

• • •

George G. George looked like his son J.G., only six inches taller, two hundred pounds heavier, and wearing a dark blue pinstripe suit. His pale blue eyes went from me to Billy, and his frowning mouth got even frownier.

"What was that!" he said.

"What was what?" Billy asked.

"I heard a dog bark!" he barked.

"That was me," I said, thinking quickly. "I was practicing my animal imitations."

George George nailed me with his steely gaze. "You are that Crump girl!"

He had me there. I was that Crump girl.

"You're the one who got my son into trouble!"

"Me?" I was too astonished to say anything else.

Billy came to my rescue. "Dad, I explained to you. Ginger didn't do anything wrong. She even helped me figure out how to undo the SCIC thing. Anyway, it was J.G. who stole the Projac. I just confiscated it from his room. And none of it would have happened if he hadn't glued my nose shut in the first place."

George George swiveled his gaze back to Billy. "You blame everything on your brother! I'll have you know he was voted the most popular boy in his class!"

"That's because everybody was afraid to vote against him."

George G. George scowled. It was a fearsome scowl, and I'm sure he used it at work to terrify ACPOD employees—including my dad—but it was all I could do to keep a straight face, because I was imagining him wearing pink polka-dot boxers.

"Hrumph!" he said, then wheeled and walked back up the stairs.

"Sorry about that," Billy said to me.

"It's okay," I said. "He kind of reminds me of my mom."

27

Agent Ffelps

When I got home an hour later, a man wearing a black suit was sitting in our living room drinking ginkgo tea with my mother. My mom is crazy for ginkgo tea.

"Ginger, this is Agent Ffelps," said my mother. "With two *f*'s. He's with the Department of Homeland Security."

Agent Ffelps smiled. He had a piece of gingko leaf stuck to his front tooth.

"Good afternoon, Mr. Ffelps," I said.

"Good afternoon, young lady," he said with the smarmy sort of smile that adults who aren't around kids much think is friendly and reassuring, but really it's just flat-out creepy.

"Excuse me," I said, and went to throw my bag of dirty clothes down the laundry chute. Mom stopped me with her voice.

"Ginger, dear, Agent Ffelps would like to have a word with you."

"About what?"

"Don't be rude. Come over here and sit down."

I came over there and sat down, carrying my bag of stinky clothes. Ffelps turned up the wattage on his phony smile.

"Your mother tells me you had a visitor this morning."

I did my best to act innocent and bewildered.

"A dog?" Ffelps prompted.

"Oh," I said. "The *dog*. I thought you meant a person. That's usually what people mean when they say 'You had a visitor.'"

"Your mother tells me this dog was somewhat unusual."

"I thought you guys were supposed to be protecting us from terrorists and illegal aliens and stuff," I said. "Are you working for Animal Control now?"

Agent Ffelps chuckled. "Heh-heh-heh." It was the fakiest chuckle I'd ever heard.

"Our national security is everybody's job," he said. It sounded as if he was reading it off a poster.

"Is this dog a terrorist?" I said.

Instead of answering my question, he pulled out his phone and put it on the coffee table between us. I could see that it was set to record.

"Tell me about the dog," he said, smiling his smarmy smile.

I tried to mimic his smile. "The *terrorist* dog?"

My mother said, "Ginger. Please."

"He was a basset hound," I said.

Ffelps nodded eagerly to show how delighted he was with my cooperation.

"He was wearing this funny collar. It had a miniature recorder on it so that you think the dog is talking. One of those practical-joke things? Like a whoopee cushion?"

"Yes, yes, exactly!" Ffelps was pleased with my line of thought.

"Anyway, I found the switch on it and turned it off. Then I went to take the dog over to Myke Duchakis's, because Myke likes animals. So I figured it might be his dog."

"The dog is with this, er, Myke Duchakis?"

"Actually, I never got there. We were going past the park and the stupid dog took off after a squirrel. I tried to catch him, but he got away. That was the last I saw of him."

Agent Ffelps sighed deeply to let me know how disappointed he was in me.

"You should have had him on a leash," he said.

"I did."

"Then how did he get away from you?"

"His stupid collar snapped."

That revived him. "You mean you still have the collar?"

"Not exactly." I was going to make him work for it.

"Well? Do you have it or don't you?" Ffelps asked.

"No."

He looked to my mom for help, but all he got was a little shrug and a helpless smile. She didn't like this Agent Ffelps-with-two-*f*'s either.

"What do you mean, 'No'?" he asked me.

"I mean no, I don't have the collar."

"Then where is it?"

"Agent Ffelps," said my mother in her most chilling witch-queen voice, "I will thank you not to shout at my daughter."

Ffelps recoiled as if he'd been slapped. Mom can have that effect on people.

"I didn't . . . I wasn't . . ."

I took pity on him.

"Look, a collar's no good without a dog, right? Besides, I tried turning the switch on and off, but the recorder or whatever wasn't working. So . . ."

"So?" He almost screeched.

"So I threw it away."

Ffelps's eyes bulged. "Threw . . . it . . . *away*?"

"Away. It was broken."

"Where?" Realizing that he had screeched, he

looked fearfully at my mother, who bestowed upon him her iciest stare. "I mean, where did you leave the collar?" he said quietly.

"In a trash can, of course. I'm not a litterbug."

"What trash can?"

I told him.

28

Ruff! Roof!

Except I didn't tell him *exactly*.

I told him I'd thrown the collar into a trash can in Flinkwater Park.

"Where? Which one?"

"I don't remember," I said. "Just some random can."

Ffelps was on his phone in a split nanosecond, then out the door without so much as a *Thank you for the ginkgo tea, Mrs. Crump.*

The door slammed, and my mother looked at me with one perfectly plucked eyebrow perfectly arched, silently inquiring as to what had *really* happened with Redge and his collar.

"You don't want to know," I said.

I heard later that the DHS descended on Flinkwater Park like a horde of black-suited raccoons, upending every one of the fifty-odd trash receptacles and sorting through the bottles, cans, picnic scraps, and bags of dog poop. Naturally, I had put the collar in the last trash can they would check—the one in the women's restroom. They did find it eventually, and although the collar was no longer functional, I'm sure they were relieved to know that it had not fallen into the hands of terrorists.

I also heard that two of the DHS agents spotted a tall, ragged, manlike creature running through the woods. They pursued the strange beast but were unable to capture it. For the past several days DHS teams, outfitted in SWAT gear and full camouflage, have been combing the park in search of the Flinkwater Sasquatch.

But they never did get catch it. Or Redge.

That night Myke and I sneaked out after midnight and met Billy and Redge at the culvert down by the river. We walked Redge up to the overpass, where a pickup truck driven by one Gerald Ruff, roofing contractor, was waiting. Redge hopped into the cab of the truck without hesitating. He was so glad to be out of that sewer he would have gone with anybody.

"Remember," I said, "keep him out of sight for a few weeks. And give him a new name."

"Don't worry," said Gerald Ruff. He reached over and scratched the dog's ears. "How about I call you Ruffie, boy? You like that?"

"Ruff! Roof!" Redge barked.

Gerald Ruff beamed.

"A talking dog," he said. "Who'da thunk it?"

Episode Three

The Zealous Zombie

29

Kissless

Several days after the talking-dog incident, at precisely 6:12 a.m., I was lying awake in bed considering a somewhat disturbing factoid. Before the end of the summer I would officially turn fourteen, and I had never kissed a boy.

I had done my research. The first kiss is an important milestone in a young woman's journey through life—a special moment that deserves to be enjoyed and treasured for all her days on earth. My week of being grounded was finally over, and I could see no reason to delay. By the end of the day, I decided, I would be kissed.

I did not realize at the time that my plans would be ruined by a foul-mouthed monkey, the Department of Homeland Security, and a zombie.

First thing I did when I got up was to make a flowchart.

1) Identify Kissable Boy

2) Find Romantic Kissing Spot

3) Lure Kissable Boy to Kissing Spot

4) Employ Feminine Charms

5) Place lips in approximate vicinity of Kissable Boy's lips

6) Close eyes (or not—in movies they usually close their eyes, but it seemed silly to experience such an Important Milestone in a state of blindness)

7) Experience First Kiss (with or without eyes open)

8) Treasure First Kiss for all of Eternity

Step 1 was easy—only one boy met my requirements: Billy George, my future husband. I'd been thinking about kissing him for a very long time.

Steps 2 through 8 were less certain, especially step 4, the part where I had to make Billy *want* to kiss me. The problem was that to Billy, the big-chested avatars on his tablet were just as real as my slight-chested flesh-and-blood self. Which put me at a disadvantage.

I am very observant, however, and I was aware of the many enticement techniques that have been practiced by women ever since we were living in caves. You know, the lipstick, the eyelash batting, hair touching, perfume wearing, cleavage exposing, and so forth. Such strategies might seem rather blatant, but where Billy was concerned, the more blatant the better. I might even have to resort to extreme measures, like cornering him and saying "Kiss me or else"—a tactic of last resort. But I wasn't ruling it out.

I needed practice. A beta test, as engineers like to say.

I'd been meaning to visit Myke Duchakis anyway. I hadn't seen him since we'd saved Redge from being euthanized, and I was wondering what he was up to. Probably plotting to free the rest of the experimental animals in Area 51.

His mother answered the door and looked me up and down, checking to make sure I wasn't smuggling in another orphaned creature.

"Heavens, don't you look . . . special!" she said.

I had done a little work on myself. Specifically, I had put on a tasteful amount of lipstick and a touch of eyeliner. Maybe more than a touch. And I was wearing a scoop neck T-shirt that showed a bit more of my upper chest than usual—

Mrs. Duchakis leaned toward me and sniffed. "You smell nice too," she observed.

—and a generous dab of my mother's perfume.

"Is Myke home?" I asked.

She regarded me with a sad little frown, then sighed and stepped aside.

"Lord save us from hormones," she muttered as I went past her and headed for the menagerie.

30

Stinky No-Tail

My plan was to get Myke to *try* to kiss me. I would then fend him off at the last instant, apologize, and call my beta test a success. Is that cruel? Yes, but this was important. My biological clock was ticking.

Myke was sprawled on the floor of his bedroom menagerie watching his chinchilla roll around in a clear plastic exercise ball. Those balls are supposed to be fun for the animal, but that chinchilla looked kind of frantic if you ask me.

"Hey," I said, willing Myke to look at me.

"Hey," he said, not looking up.

The room smelled even more animally than I remembered. I moved closer so that he could get a whiff of my perfume.

"Stupid stinky no-tail."

"What did you say?" I said, giving him one

second to apologize before I clobbered him.

"I didn't say anything," Myke said. He pointed to a cage on the top shelf. "He did."

"Ugly naked face," said the monkey in the cage.

Or rather, that's what came out of the collar around his neck.

"Give me peanut. I throw poop at you."

I said, "Mykey . . . you raided Area Fifty-One again?"

"Nope," Myke said. "That's the same monkey I told you about before—the one Redge chased out of the building. Don't get too close. He's not kidding about throwing poop."

"Yuck! What's he doing *here*?"

"Making my life miserable." He stood up, took a peanut from his pocket, and held it out to the monkey. A tiny hand darted between the bars and snatched it.

"Ha-ha, stupid no-tail, I steal your peanut!"

"I mean, how did he *get* here?"

"Oh. I found him. I was worried about him. I thought, if I was a monkey and I escaped from a top secret laboratory, where would I go?"

I looked at him blankly. I had no idea where a monkey would go.

"To the nearest trees!" he said.

"Oh." I guess it was obvious.

"Area Fifty-One is only a hundred yards from Flinkwater Park. I went there with a bag of peanuts and a cage. Sure enough, Dipwad showed up."

"You call him *Dipwad*?"

"It's nicer than what *he* calls *me*."

"Ugly stinky no-tail, I eat your peanut! Ha-ha-ha-ha-ha!" Dipwad bared his sharp little teeth and threw the empty shell at us.

"How did you catch him?"

"I put some peanuts in the cage and waited for him to go in. He's really not very smart."

"Smell like bad food rotten stinky stupid poop."

"Is this how all monkeys think?"

Myke shrugged and sat down on the edge of his bed.

"Why don't you turn off his collar?"

"He bites."

"They're going to want the monkey back just as bad as they wanted Redge. You could get in serious trouble!"

"I don't think so," he said. "There were a lot of monkeys there. They probably don't even realize he's gone."

"They will."

He shrugged. "I guess."

"What are you going to do?"

"Peanut! Peanut! Ugly no-tail give peanut!"

Myke, looking miserable, said "Wait for the battery to run out?"

I had picked a bad time to practice my feminine

wiles on Myke Duchakis. But since I'd gone to all the trouble of putting on makeup and perfume, I thought I'd make an effort. If I could break through Myke's monkey-induced misery, it would prove that my strategy was effective.

I sat down next to him on the bed. This was not such a provocative act as you may think—Myke's bed was strewn with boxes and plastic tubs of several varieties of animal food for his chinchilla, his mice, his pigeon, his three-legged squirrel, and his leopard gecko. There were also several peanut shells, presumably flung there by Dipwad. It was about as romantic as a landfill.

I said, "Myke."

He looked at me. "Do you have a cold?"

"No! Why?"

"Your voice sounds weird."

So much for my attempt at talking sexy-sultry. I tried batting my eyes.

"Do you have something in your eye?"

I played with my hair and giggled.

"What's so funny?" he asked.

"You're an idiot," I said.

"Huh?"

"Kiss me," I said, resorting to more direct tactics.

"Why would I do that?"

I clobbered him.

• • •

Okay, all I did, really, was punch him on the shoulder and stomp out of the room.

"Dear Lord, is everything all right?" Mrs. Duchakis inquired.

"Do you know that there are *two* lower primates in there?" I said.

Looking back, that may have been a mistake. Myke probably didn't want his mom to know about the monkey. But I was in no mood for intelligent decisions.

31

Grey Goo

It was only ten in the morning, and my plan was already falling apart, all because of that stupid monkey. I hadn't even gotten to step 2: Find Romantic Kissing Spot.

I knew one thing for sure. The event could not take place in Billy's sanctuary, or anywhere with a working tablet in view. I refused to compete with a warrior-queen avatar. It would have to be someplace quiet, private, and most important, *romantic*.

Unfortunately, such places were in short supply in Flinkwater. All I could think of was Jerry's Custard, the ice cream shop on Old Main Street. It was not particularly quiet, private, or romantic—but they did have an *amazing* maple caramel crisp custard, and I knew that was one thing that would get Billy out of his boy cave. I sent him a text.

Maple Caramel Crisp Custard. Now.

It took him a minute to respond.

Can't. Nanolab.

Nanolab? It was summer break—why would he be going to school?

???????????????

His answer came back instantly.

Grey goo!!!

Grey goo?

I knew what grey goo was, of course. I mean, who doesn't know about grey goo?

Sorry—I am making assumptions. Maybe you slept through that part of your nanotech class.

I am being sarcastic again.

You know what a nanobot is, right? Short for nanorobot? A very small robot? Smaller than the diameter of a human hair? Smaller even than the smallest thing visible to the human eye? Well, now you know.

Most nanobots are pretty simple. Billy and I had been lab partners last spring, and we'd built our own bot. All it did was roll around in a circle—not terribly useful—but it was still pretty cool. Some advanced nanobots are already being used to treat diseases such as cancer. But nanorobotics is still in its infancy, and the reason for *that* can be summed up in two words: "grey goo."

Imagine you built a nanobot whose only job was to build more tiny nanobots exactly like itself. And that all the baby robots did exactly the same thing—build more identical robots. And imagine that these self-replicating, invisibly small bots had unlimited access to energy and materials. What you would have is an ever-growing mass of nanobots consuming everything in their path. Eventually they might cover the entire surface of the earth in—you guessed it—grey goo.

Nobody wants that to happen, so nanobot researchers tend to be very cautious.

Of course, no one has ever actually *made* a perpetually self-replicating nanobot. Even if you did make one, it would quickly run out of food or energy. In practice, grey goo is impossible.

Which is what they used to say about human flight.

So who knows? In any case, I knew that Billy would not be able to resist going over to the school to check it out. *Grey goo!* To him that would be the coolest thing ever—right up there with aliens landing in Flinkwater. Or the sun going nova.

I just might be able to compete with a warrior-queen avatar, but grey goo was like the Unholy Grail of nanotech. If I wanted to get kissed by Billy, I would have to go to the Flinkwater High School nanotech laboratory.

32

"The Monkey
Is on the Move"

On my way to the high school I counted three black SUVs. Were they watching me, or was this a normal variation in their patrol routine?

It may be that I noticed the DHS more than most people due to the fact that Agent Ffelps had taken a personal interest in me. Billy had the same problem—a black SUV was parked permanently outside his house. If he wanted to get out without being seen, he had to take the sewer route.

My dad said we were being monitored extra closely because our parents were Assets of Critical Importance. George G. George was the acting president of ACPOD, my dad was Director of Cyber-Security Services, and my mom was the Human Resources Director. Also, I think Agent Ffelps was still convinced that Billy and I were terrorists, which was why I wasn't too surprised when one of the SUVs pulled over and two guys in dark suits jumped out and accosted me.

Okay, maybe "accosted" is too strong. I could say they "invited" me to step into the vehicle. In any case, I found myself sitting in the back of a government SUV facing a smarmily smiling Agent Ffelps.

"Good morning, Mr. Ffelps," I said.

"Good morning, Ginger," said Agent Ffelps.

"What can I do for you?" I asked sweetly.

"I'm looking for a monkey," he said smarmily.

"Have you experimented with mirrors?" Since my mom wasn't there, I did not feel the need to be so polite.

Ffelps did his scripted laugh: "Heh-heh-heh."

"We know you were just visiting Mycroft Duchakis," he said.

That threw me for a second.

"Oh, you mean Mykey?"

"Yes. The boy with all the animals."

I waited for him to continue.

"You didn't happen to see a monkey while you were there, did you?"

"I'm not sure," I said. "He has a lot of animals."

"So I have heard. We're awaiting a search warrant. I thought perhaps you could illuminate us in the interim."

"Illuminate? Interim?"

Agent Ffelps sighed, longly and loudly. Try it sometime. It's not easy.

"Ginger," he said, "I like you."

I did not return the compliment.

"But this is not a game. We are dealing with national security here."

"I thought we were dealing with monkeys."

Ffelps touched a hand to his ear, tipped his head, frowned, nodded, frowned some more. For a moment I thought he was having a seizure, then I realized he was wearing a receiver in his ear.

He spoke into his lapel. "Seal the perimeter; I'm on my way." He turned to the driver. "The monkey is on the move."

I laughed. He gave me a questioning look.

"What you just said," I said.

"Get out," said Ffelps.

33

Moles

Flinkwater High School is next door to the ACPOD campus. In the morning the ACPOD corporate tower sends its long, ominous shadow creeping over the school building. Mrs. Singh, my English teacher, claims that's a metaphor, but I attribute it to plain old bad planning.

Since I had been delayed by Agent Ffelps, I wasn't sure if I'd arrived before Billy. I tried the front door. It was unlocked. I stepped inside.

I had never before been in the school when it wasn't full of students. It was eerily empty, and not at all romantic. I stood there for a few seconds, undecided. Should I wait for Billy, or go straight to the nanolab? The door opened behind me, and I think my heart stopped. I spun around. It was Billy.

"Are you okay?" he said.

"I'm fine. You just startled me."

He cocked his head. "You look different."

Giving him the benefit of the doubt, I smiled and said, "Thank you."

"Your lips are kind of red."

"That's called lipstick."

"Oh. How come you're wearing lipstick?"

"Because I'm a girl?"

"Oh," he said, blinking in apparent astonishment.

This first-kiss business was going to be more work than I'd thought.

"So . . . you said something about grey goo?" I asked.

"I was kidding," he said. "Professor Little called. He said he needed an assistant to help him with a self-replicating nanobot he was designing. He was pretty excited."

"But . . . isn't that kind of dangerous? Like, turn-the-planet-into-a-giant-ball-of-grey-goo dangerous?"

"I'm sure the professor has plenty of safety protocols in place to prevent *that* from happening."

"We're talking about a teacher who once showed up for class wearing SpongeBob SquarePants pajamas," I said doubtfully. "Why did he call you, anyway?"

"We've been working on some things."

"Grey goo things?"

"Well . . . not exactly. You know he's been work-ing on some antitumor nanotech, right?"

I didn't, but I nodded.

"He—we, actually—came up with a variation on a self-replicator that attacked a certain kind of growth. Specifically, melanocytic nevi."

"Melano . . . what?"

"Moles."

"I see," I said.

34

In the Dark

Professor Lancaster Little, our nanotech teacher and a researcher for ACPOD, was one of the ugliest human beings I had ever met. Physically, I mean. As a person, Professor Little was quite nice—albeit a tad absentminded. But he had several large, unfortunately positioned moles. The biggest one was the size and color of a grape, and it was situated on the tip of his nose. It was impossible to look at anything else. Even if you were able to tear your eyes away from that supermole, they would land on one of the other moles, like the double mole on his chin, or the one hanging off his left eyelid, or the constellation of moles decorating the top of his mostly bald head.

Don't get me wrong, I *liked* Professor Little. I just had a really hard time *looking* at him. It made perfect sense that he would try to develop some antimole nanotech.

"The professor said he had a breakthrough," Billy said as we walked down the hallway. "He asked me to stop by the nanolab."

"To help him get rid of his moles?" I said, still trying to wrap my head around the idea.

"I don't think we're quite to that point yet. The nanobots haven't been tested."

"So we're not about to perish in a sea of grey goo?"

"Well, no. At least I don't think so."

I figured that once we had to look at Professor Little's face it would kill any chance of romance, so as we were passing by the school theater, I moved closer to Billy.

"Listen," I whispered.

"Why?" he said. His voice boomed through the hallway.

"Shhh!"

"What? There's nobody here."

"I know. It's kind of scary." I grabbed his hand.

"Ouch," he said.

"Ouch?"

"Your fingers are digging into me."

Boys are weird.

I said, "You know what would be exciting?"

"A self-replicating nanobot?"

"No. The theater. With nobody in it. Except us."

"Why would that be exciting?"

"It just would." I pulled him toward the theater entrance. Rather to my surprise, he followed.
I pushed the door open and we stepped inside. The
door swung shut behind us.

It was completely, totally black.

"Wow," Billy said. "This *is* cool!"

What I had in mind: the two of us, sitting cozily in
an empty theater, looking up at the empty stage,
with no sound but our own breathing. I thought it
would be exciting in a romantic sort of way.

Utter, mind-numbing blackness is not romantic.

"I don't like this," I said darkly.

"Then why did you drag me in here?"

"Never mind." I backed up until my butt hit
the door and pushed back through into the hallway.
"Come on," I said. "Grey goo awaits."

35

Nanobots

The Flinkwater High School nanotech laboratory was not a serious ACPOD-level research facility, but it was advanced way beyond an Easy-Bake Oven and a couple of test tubes. We had a sterile build-box with a digital electron microscope, and a set of computer-assisted hydrogen-fiber waldoes that could manipulate matter on a near-molecular level.

"Why is the professor working here at the school?" I asked. "Doesn't he have access to the ACPOD labs?"

"He quit ACPOD a few months ago," Billy said. "He said he didn't like what they were doing to animals over in Area Fifty-One."

The door to the nanolab was locked, as usual. Billy pressed the buzzer. Nobody answered.

"That's strange," Billy said. "He told me he'd

be here." He pulled something out of his pocket. It looked like a deck of miniature playing cards.

"What are those for?" I asked.

"Key cards," he said as he sorted through them.

"That's a lot of key cards."

"You never know when you might have to open something. This one is the key to my dad's office. And this one is the bank."

"The *bank*?"

"Yeah. Here's the key to the police station, and this one's the master key for all the school locks. Watch."

He swiped the key across the sensor. The nano-lab door opened with a sucking, hissing sound. The high school nanotech lab might not be a serious research facility, but it still had some serious safety features—like negative air pressure and a pneu-matically sealed door—to ensure that no rogue nanobots escaped.

Inside the lab the air felt still and dead.

"Professor Little?" Billy called out.

Silence.

"Weird."

The build-box display was turned on. Billy sat down at the controls and zoomed in on the image—a glass petri dish containing a reddish, gooey-looking ball no larger than a pea.

The build-box controller had a seat large

enough to accommodate two people, like a love seat, only without the arms, back, and cushions. Okay, like a bench. I sat down beside Billy. Our shoulders were touching. He didn't seem to notice.

He zoomed in some more. "Look, they're moving."

The surface of the ball of red goo was shifting and writhing in a most unsettling way.

"Those are nanobots?" I asked.

"Yeah. Probably about a million of them."

"How many would it take to remove a mole?"

"In theory, only one, because they're self-replicating. The idea is that you put a smear of bots on a mole. The bots recognize the abnormal flesh and start to absorb it while reproducing themselves. When they run out of mole flesh, the bots draw the normal skin together, seal it, shut themselves down, then drop off like a scab."

"Eww!"

"The professor said he was having trouble getting the bots to turn themselves off. I wonder where he is."

"He probably forgot you were coming and went home. He *is* a little absentminded."

Billy turned the monitor up to maximum magnification so that we could see the individual bots. Now they looked like a cluster of red ants crawling over each other. "They're pretty active," he said.

I leaned closer to him, pressing my shoulder against his. "What are they doing?"

"My guess is there's some energy source in the middle of that blob. Pretty soon they'll run out of food and stop moving."

"That's amazing," I said, trying to make my voice husky.

He looked at me, then drew back and said, "Do you have a cold?"

"No!"

"Your voice sounds funny."

I batted my eyes. "Billy . . . do you remember the time we spent here last spring?"

He looked blank.

"When we built the nanobot that spun around all on its own?"

"Oh!" His eyes lit up. "That was fun. You were there?"

"I was your lab partner!"

"Oh."

I pressed closer to him. "You're the smartest boy I know."

"Really?" He liked that. I could tell. I licked my lips and ran my hand through my hair and batted my eyes some more. Maybe that was too much, but I wanted to be sure he was thinking about me and not about nanobots. I tipped my head and stared into his eyes. His pupils had gotten bigger. I could smell his breath—a little peanut-buttery, but not bad.

It was working. I had hypnotized him with my feminine charms. Our faces were only about ten inches apart. Slowly, dreamlike, our lips moved closer—

"Nnngh! Urr! Gack!"

Billy and I flew apart as if the air between us had exploded.

"Hgnak! Heek! Awwng!"

We jumped to our feet and looked around wildly, searching for the source of the horrible choking, gasping noises.

"Awwwwwwnnnnnnnnn!" A groaning, gasping ginormity of a moan, like the last drawn-out gasp of a dying ogre. My heart had stopped—literally, I think—and every hair on my body was quivering.

"Did you hear that?" I whispered.

Billy, eyes wide, nodded.

36

Zombie

For a few seconds there was silence, then came a scraping, foot-dragging sound.

"I think it's coming from over there," Billy whispered, pointing at the lab bench at the far end of the room.

My mouth was too dry to speak.

Billy said, "Maybe we should get out of here."

That sounded like a good idea to me. Except I couldn't move. It was like one of those dreams where you're paralyzed—except I wasn't asleep. I just couldn't make my legs move. Billy seemed to be having the same problem.

We heard more scraping, another groaning gasp, and a creature rose up from behind the bench. It staggered to its feet and stood swaying, waving its arms and howling.

"Hwaargh! Ghurk!"

I knew what it was right away by its staggering gait and the horrible sounds. But most of all I knew it from the red, oozing wounds covering its ruin of a face.

"Zombie!" I screamed.

Billy was screaming too, and suddenly we were both running for the door.

The zombie came after us, grunting and groaning, its limbs flailing spastically. Billy and I grabbed the door handle at the same moment—but the door wouldn't budge. It took a second for me to realize that I was pulling while Billy was pushing, but when I switched to pushing he started pulling. Behind us, the zombie let out a horrific shriek. I looked back just as it fell face-first to the floor, writhing and wriggling and moaning piteously.

Billy let go of the door handle. I pushed the door open.

"Come *on*!" I yelled.

"No, wait! Look at what it's wearing."

I looked.

Then I looked again.

"Are those *SpongeBob* pajamas?" I asked.

Billy stepped toward him.

"Don't let him bite you!" I said.

Billy said, "Professor Little?"

"*Hrawnnnnn!*" said the zombie version of Professor Little.

"It's okay!" Billy said, moving toward him. "It's just nanobots."

"Nanobots turn people into zombies?"

"No! Come here, help me."

The zombie professor was having some sort of seizure. Billy—my hero—stuck his hand in the professor's mouth and pulled out a gob of the most disgusting red goo imaginable. The professor coughed and sprayed red glop all over Billy's face. Billy wiped it away like it was nothing. The professor gasped and spat and coughed and spat some more, sending my yuck-meter dials spinning out of control.

"Professor! Are you okay?" Billy shouted.

The professor sat up and shook his head violently. Bits of red came flying off him, including one largish blob that had been attached to the tip of his nose.

The only reason I didn't run off screaming right then was because Billy—my hero—seemed so calm.

"Thank you, my boy," said Professor Little in a hoarse voice. More of the red glop was falling from his face and hands. "I don't suppose you could get me a towel?"

Billy ran over to the towel dispenser and came back with a wad of paper towels. The professor began to wipe his face clean, and I noticed a remarkable thing.

The grape-size mole on his nose was gone. And so were all his other lumps, blobs, and blotches.

"Well?" he said. "How do I look?"

37

Affianced

We took a moment to marvel at the new, mole-free Professor Little. Billy said, "You look great, Professor. Just a little shiny is all."

He *did* look shiny. As if somebody had stretched his skin tight over his head and then buffed it to a waxy sheen. Except for the peculiar texture, he was not a bad-looking man. If he'd had any hair on the top of his head he might have been quite handsome.

The professor tried to smile. His skin stretched.

"It feels a little tight," he said. "But I suppose that's only to be expected. The treatment removes the nevi, but it doesn't make new skin. In time, the epidermis will grow and relax." The professor climbed to his feet. More reddish clumps of nanoglop dropped to the floor. I stepped back to avoid them.

"Don't worry," he said. "The bots have gone dormant."

"What happened?" Billy asked.

"A slight miscalculation is all." The professor brushed the last of the glop from his pajamas. "I underestimated the number of melanocytic nevi present, and the nanos . . . well, I guess they got a little overexcited." He walked over to a small mirror hanging on the wall and examined his reflection. "But it worked!"

"But Professor, why would you test it out on yourself?" I asked.

"To get rid of my nevi, of course!" he said, admiring his shiny, tight new features.

"Yeah, but wouldn't it have made more sense to first try it out on, I don't know, a moley mouse or something?"

The professor stiffened. "I would *never* experiment on a helpless animal! That was why I resigned my position at ACPOD. They wanted me to inject experimental nanotech into a monkey. I refused, of course."

"Of course," I said, thinking of Dipwad.

"Also, I was in a bit of a hurry," the professor said. "I'm getting married, you see."

"Married?"

"Yes. My fiancée will be flying in from Schenectady this very afternoon."

"And—what? You wanted to surprise her?"

"That is precisely what I *didn't* want to do. You see, Hillary and I have never met. Face to face, that is."

"You're marrying somebody you don't know?"

"Oh, we've had an online relationship for several months."

"But you've never *seen* each other?"

"Of course we've seen each other. We make video calls all the time. She's a lovely woman. Gorgeous, in fact. Only—perhaps it was dishonest of me—I used a little visual enhancement program on my own image. I, um, I may have edited out certain aspects of my facial features."

38

TSA

An hour later the three of us were standing in the waiting area at the Flinkwater County Airport. The professor had on a slightly threadbare but clean herringbone sport coat with leather patches on the elbows. I'd helped him pick it out from the pathetic selection hanging in his closet. He looked quite handsome—in a shiny, balding, twitchy, absentminded professor sort of way.

Billy was more interested in airport technology than in the human drama about to unfold. He was watching people make their way through the security gate.

"I bet I could make a bomb that those security scanners could never detect," he said.

"Why would you do that?" I asked.

"I wouldn't. I'm just saying I *could*. If I wanted to."

The people coming from the gate area were the usual assortment of Flinkwater visitors—several engineer-types and a few sales-types. I knew which one was Hillary the moment she appeared: perfect hair, bright red lipstick, dressed to kill, and visibly nervous. She stepped tentatively into the waiting area, her eyes quickly scanning the people there, skittering past us, doing a double take, then fixing upon the professor. She smiled uncertainly, then came toward us. As she got closer, I noticed something else about her.

An enormous purple mole bulged from the point of her chin. It could have competed with the professor's now-missing nose bauble.

I looked at the professor. He was staring wide-eyed at his approaching fiancée. I held my breath. The professor held out his arms and moved toward her. They embraced, then looked happily into each other's eyes.

"Hilly-poo," said Professor Little.

"Lankydoodle," said Hilly-poo.

I looked at Billy and mouthed, *Lankydoodle?* He rolled his eyes.

Hilly-poo's eyes were wet. She blinked, and tears streamed down her cheeks.

"I am so sorry!" she exclaimed, pushing herself away.

"Sorry for what?" the professor asked, bewildered.

She raised a hand and touched the mole hanging from her chin. "I didn't want you to see this. I've been editing it out of our video calls. I'd planned to have it removed, but the doctor said it was too big. He said it would require major surgery. But I will! I will have it removed, my love!"

The professor was staring at her mole with a delighted expression on his shiny face.

"Dear one," he said, "I love your little melanocytic nevus. But if you don't want it, perhaps you will allow me to show you a little something I've been working on in my laboratory."

"Oh Lankydoodle!"

"Hilly-poo!"

And then they kissed.

I must confess to having mixed feelings at that moment. On the one hand, this was some serious romance—the lonely, previously mole-ridden professor and the lonely, presently mole-ridden lady from Schenectady find each other and kiss for the first time. I suspected it was the first time *ever* for the professor. I mean, I was tearing up a little.

On the other hand, it reminded me of my own never-been-kissed situation. I turned toward

Billy, wondering if I had the courage to plant a big smooch on him right then and there, but Billy was over by the security gate, talking to one of the TSA agents. Then there were two agents talking to him. Suddenly two more TSA agents rushed over, took Billy by his arms, and marched him toward a door marked SECURITY ONLY.

"Hey!" I yelled, running toward them.

Another agent—a woman the size of a gorilla—grabbed me around the waist and lifted me off the floor.

"Billy!" I shouted. He looked back at me, his eyes wide, as they shunted him into the security room. The door closed.

"Where are they taking him?" I asked Ms. Gorilla.

She set me down. "That your boyfriend?" she inquired.

"My fiancé, actually," I said.

"Is that a fact?" She seemed amused.

"You can't just go around grabbing people," I said.

"Actually, we can. Especially when they start talking about bombs in airports."

"Billy is *not* a bomber!"

"That may be, but he just boasted that he knew how to get a bomb through security."

"That doesn't make him a bomber!"

"We'll see about that. After we talk to him for a while."

"How long is 'a while'?"

"I wouldn't wait, if I were you."

Defeated, I turned back to the professor and his fiancée—but they were gone. The absent-minded Professor Little had forgotten all about me and Billy. No doubt he was on his way to the nanolab to help Hilly-poo get rid of her moley-poo.

Thirteen going on fourteen, I was stuck at the airport with no one to kiss.

39

"Right on the Kisser"

I had to take a cab back to town. I told myself not to be too worried about Billy. They'd just ask him a bunch of questions and make him sit there for a few hours, then send him home. At least I hoped so—he hadn't actually *done* anything.

The cabbie drove me to an address on Elm Avenue. I paid him with the last of the credit balance on my phone and got out. A black SUV pulled over a few car lengths behind us. It had been following us ever since we left the airport. DHS? TSA? Men in Black? Maybe they were all the same—it didn't matter. I had a mission to complete.

I walked through a toy-strewn front yard up to a small bungalow and rang the bell. The door was answered by my aunt Janet, carrying my six-month-old cousin Melanie on her hip.

"Ginger! How nice to see you! What are you doing on this side of town?"

"I was in the neighborhood," I said.

"Come in!"

My aunt Janet really likes having babies. In addition to Melanie, she has a set of eighteen-month-old twin boys, and her oldest child, Kellan, age two years and nine months. The moment I stepped inside, I heard the sound of a stamping toddler. An instant later Kellan came charging into the living room wearing nothing but a pair of disposable diapers decorated with, of all things, SpongeBob SquarePants.

"Gineeeeeeeee!" he shrieked, throwing himself at me. I caught him and almost fell over backward. He was getting big!

"Guess what!" he yelled in my face.

"Um . . . you found out you have a super loud voice?"

"No! I pooped all by myself!"

I laughed. "That's great, kiddo. Now how about you give your cousin Ginger a great big smooch?" I pointed at my lips. "Right on the kisser."

Episode Four

The Secretive Sasquatch

40

Gilly

The walk home was almost a mile, and there was never a moment when that black SUV let me out of sight. They didn't even try to be sneaky about it, and they never offered me a lift.

I wondered how Billy was doing, so I called him as I was walking up River Street and got a recorded message that his number was not available. Then I called Myke to find out what had happened to the talking monkey. Same story: number not available.

This was getting seriously weird. The SUV was still creeping along half a block behind me. I wanted to make a rude gesture. Then I thought about Billy being dragged off by those TSA agents, and I decided not to.

Paranoid? Maybe a little. Not necessarily a bad thing, according to Uncle Ashton. He once told me, "Paranoid ain't paranoid if they're really after you. It's a survival skill."

I decided to ditch them. I ducked into the alleyway behind the Jensens' house and took off running. The SUV followed me into the alley, but not before I'd climbed over the Jensens' fence and run through their backyard. Before the SUV could back out of the alley, I dashed across Seventh Street, cut through several backyards, followed the railroad tracks to the Ninth Street trestle bridge, then headed for home, taking a circuitous route through the neighborhood and letting myself in the back door.

Professional antiterrorist agents are no match for a girl who knows every square inch of Flinkwater.

I could hear my parents talking in the front room. Why weren't they at work? I heard another voice too—one I didn't recognize. Since I was already in stealth mode, I sneaked down the hall and peeked into the living room.

Mom and Dad were sitting on the living room sofa. Sitting across from them, in my dad's favorite chair, was an extraordinarily hairy man wearing ragged, camouflage bib overalls and a dark green flannel shirt.

Let me tell you how hairy the hairy man was. Neanderthal hairy. Chewbacca hairy. Five years since his last shave or haircut hairy. Thick, graying hair spiraled out from his head, forming a crown of tangled dreadlocks. An equally snarled and knotted beard began high on his cheeks and ran all the way down his neck. Even the backs of his hands were as hairy as hobbit feet.

The creature sitting in my dad's easy chair was, without a doubt, the Flinkwater Sasquatch.

I remember the first time my cat encountered a DustBot. We had just picked Barney up from the shelter, and he wasn't much more than a kitten. Of course he immediately began exploring every square centimeter of his new home, and the first thing he saw was one of our gerbil-size DustBots crawling along the edge of the living room carpet. His ears went up, his tail puffed out, and his eyes got huge. But he didn't run away. He was scared, but his curiosity canceled out the scaredy-cat in him, and he began to stalk the strange, humming creature. It took him a few minutes, but finally he got up the courage to thwap it with his paw and flip it onto its back.

That was how I felt. The Sasquatch, naturally, scared the heck out of me. But my curiosity kept me rooted to the spot.

My dad was talking.

". . . keep asking about the NLP protocols developed by our kinesthetics division for something they're cooking up over in Area Fifty-One. The DHS has their people monitoring every department.

I can't even wash my hands without a DHS agent looking over my shoulder. It's as if the government has taken over ACPOD, and—"

The Sasquatch interrupted. "ACPOD is a private company and under no obligation to cooperate with any government agency." His voice was surprisingly soft.

"Unless they declare martial law," said my mother.

"Which is what they did after the SCIC incident, Gil," said my father. "But even after we solved the SCIC problem, they didn't *undeclare* it. There are more than a hundred DHS agents here. George George has essentially given them the keys to ACPOD."

"Unacceptable!" said the Sasquatch. "Impossible! Egregious! Unspeakable! Intolerable! Incon—"

"Gilly!" My mother cut him off.

"Sorry."

"The point is, Gil, you have to step in," my dad said. "No one else has the authority to overrule George. And we need to take this public—let people know that their government is using these strong-arm tactics on a private company for no good reason."

"I . . . can't," said the Sasquatch known as Gil.

"Why not? You're still the majority shareholder, chairman of the board in absentia, and the company founder."

My heart went *thud*, then it went *ka-thump*, and for a few seconds I thought I might pass out. Gil? Short for Gilbert, as in Gilbert Bates, the reclusive and missing-for-ten-years founder and genius behind ACPOD Industries? One of the smartest and richest men in the whole *world*? In our *living* room? The *Sasquatch of Flinkwater Park*?

And my mom calls him *Gilly*?

As I was having my moment of being stunned beyond all comprehension, they'd kept on talking.

". . . it's the only way, Gil. Call some of your old congressmen friends. Call the president! Didn't you have a sleepover in the Lincoln Bedroom?"

"That was ten years ago," said Gilbert Bates. "Different president."

"Then call the new one. You don't think he'd take a phone call from the most famous missing person on the planet?"

There were several seconds of silence, then Gilbert Bates said in a small voice, "I like living in the woods."

"You can still live in the woods, Gilly," said my mom.

"Would I have to cut my hair?"

"Not if you don't—" my dad started to say, but he was cut off by my mom.

"I think a little trim would be a good idea, Gilly. You do rather resemble a Sasquatch."

I couldn't stand it anymore. Now that I knew who he was, I just had to have a closer look at the famously elusive Gilbert Bates. I was about to step into the living room when the doorbell rang. All the talking stopped. I scooted down the hall to my dad's study and closed the door. Through the window I could see two dark-suited men standing on the front steps. One of them was Agent Ffelps.

A second later the study door opened. I ducked down behind the desk.

"Wait in here, Gil," I heard my dad whisper. "We'll get rid of them." The door closed. I peeked over the top of the desk. Gilbert Bates was standing in the middle of the room looking as lost as he was hairy.

41

Cabal

I stood up. "Hey."

He jumped, saw it was me, and relaxed. A little.

"I saw you in the park," I said.

He didn't say anything.

"You're the Sasquatch, right?"

"Only in the summer." A hint of a smile peeked through his beard. "In the winter they call me the Abominable Snowman."

We stared at each other. I decided I liked him.

"Are you really Gilbert Bates?"

"Only when it can't be avoided."

"And you've been living in the park all this time?"

"On and off. I have a little ranch outside of Santa Fe. But I like Flinkwater Park. I grew up here, you know. Spent most of my childhood in those woods. Also, I can keep an eye on my baby." He sounded so normal that for a moment

I forgot that I was talking to a Sasquatch.

"Your baby?"

"ACPOD, my baby, my child, offspring, progeny, pride and joy, ankle biter, youngster . . ."

He was spinning off again.

". . . sweet pea, little one, rug rat—"

"Gilly!" I said, using my mother's technique.

He stopped.

"Why does my mom call you Gilly?" I asked.

"That was her name for me when we were dating, back in the day."

"You . . . dated . . . my *mom*?" It was flat-out impossible to imagine.

"Back in the day."

"What day was *that*?"

"We were at Stanford. It was a long time ago."

"You were in college?" I thought back to what my mother had told me a few weeks ago. "I thought she was dating Josh Stevens then."

"Josh?" Gilly gave me a sideways look and snorted. "Josh never had a chance with her." His expression softened. "Then again, neither did I, once she met your dad." He shuffled over to the window and peered out. "Those men are still here."

"My uncle Ashton says they're like ticks on a dog."

"Ashton? Ash Crump? How is he, anyway? Still a spy?"

"I *knew* it!" I said.

"Ash helped me out, back in the day. He landed us our first Pentagon contract. Six thousand SpyBots." Gilly noticed a DustBot crawling along the baseboard and smiled. "That was just after we built our first DustBot. Same basic platform, only DustBots don't hover. Or spy."

The DustBot, as I'm sure you know, was the product that put ACPOD on the map. These days just about everybody has a few of them scurrying around the house cleaning up. The bot made a right turn and began climbing up the wall.

"Josh Stevens and I were roommates, you know, back in college. He still thinks the DustBot was his idea, only he called his version the Dustbunny. I think he's still mad at me."

"Why should he care? D-Monix is just as big a company as ACPOD. Practically everybody uses D-Monix tablets and desktop computers."

"Yes, but Josh is insanely competitive. He wanted to get into robotics in the worst way, but the DustBot kicked his butt." Gilly chuckled. "That Dustbunny of his never took off."

"Was it really his idea?"

"The *idea* had been around for years. When I was a boy, there was a thing called a Roomba. A sort of self-propelled vacuum cleaner. Josh and I were both trying to develop our own cleaning bots around the same time. Josh came out with his Dustbunny first, but it was too big, too noisy, too expensive, and too rabbity. Why he made it look so much like a bunny I'll never understand. Creeped people out. I mean, who wants a house full of rabbits?"

I heard the front door close. A second later my dad came into his study.

"They're gone, Gil, but—" He did a double take. "*Ginger?* What are you doing here?"

"I, um, live here?"

"Minding your own business as usual, I see."

I shrugged. He sighed, walked over to the window, and closed the blind.

"What did they want?" I asked.

"Actually, they wanted you. I told them we had no idea where you were." He cocked his head. "Which we didn't. Where *have* you been?"

I'd been so many places that I wasn't sure how to answer him.

"Just hanging out," I said after an awkward pause.

"Yes, well, your friend Billy George has been taken into custody. As has Mycroft Duchakis. As *you* would have been, had they known you were here."

"We didn't *do* anything," I said.

"According to the agents, Billy threatened to smuggle a bomb onto an aircraft, and he had several restricted key cards on his person. And Mycroft broke into an ACPOD laboratory and stole some valuable research animals. The agents claim that you were present at both events."

"They're lying! Sort of."

He cocked his head. "Sort of?"

"Well . . . I was at the airport with Billy, but he didn't threaten to bomb anybody. He just said he knew how to get a bomb past the TSA scanners. And the monkey ran off on its own. Myke found him in the woods."

"Monkey?"

"Yeah, a talking monkey."

"That monkey's a *mean* little rascal," said Gilbert Bates.

Dad and I turned to look at him.

"You know about this monkey?" Dad said.

"I met him in the woods. He wouldn't shut up. I was glad when the boy caught him."

My mom called from out in the kitchen. "Gilly, would you care for a cup of tea?"

"Yes, please," said Gilbert Bates. "Earl Grey, hot."

My dad shook his head. "Monkeys don't talk," he said.

"Dipwad does," I said. "I met a talking dog, too."

Mom came out of the kitchen with a tea tray. "I told you about the dog, dear."

"You told me it was a stray dog with some sort of joke collar!" Dad said.

"It's no joke," I said. "The animals escaped from Area Fifty-One. They're trying to control animals like they're robots."

They all stared at me.

Gilly said, "Impossible. I shut down that animal research program ten years ago. It was cruel. Not to mention unusual."

"Well, it's not shut down anymore."

Dad said, "Are you saying that ACPOD is making talking animals? How do you know this, Ginger?"

"Myke's dad is on the research team."

Gilly and my dad sat in stunned silence as Mom poured us cups of tea. She sat down and said, "You see, Gilly? You have to return to ACPOD and take charge. Flinkwater is about to be overrun with talking monkeys."

Gilly sighed and sank lower in his seat. "I fear you are right."

My dad turned to me and said, "Since you seem to have become both a fugitive and a capable spy, Ginger, I suppose we must invite you to join our little cabal."

Cabal! I liked the sound of that. Except . . . I looked at the Sasquatch.

"Do I have to go live in the woods?"

My dad laughed. "That won't be necessary . . . probably."

42

ELF

"Tell me about this Brazen Bull," said the Sasquatch as he stirred a spoonful of honey into his tea. "Since that seems to be where all this folderol started."

"What's folderol?" I asked. That was a mistake.

"Folderol, brouhaha, fuss, commotion, ballyhoo, tempest in a—"

"Gilly!" said both Mom and I at once.

"Sorry," he said. The man was a walking thesaurus.

Dad said, "We still don't understand what, exactly, caused the SCIC outbreak. I mean, we know it's somehow triggered by the visual subliminals inserted by Billy George. However, when we extract the subliminals from the program and replay them on their own, they have no effect on any of our volunteers, but when combined with the bull animation, the subliminals trigger SCIC in *one hundred percent* of our volunteers."

"It didn't affect *me*," my mom said with a hint of pride in her voice.

"Yes, not everybody who had viewed it in the wild, as it were, was affected—only seventy-two percent of the Flinkwater population who viewed the animation got bonked."

"I looked at the screenie on Theo Winkleman's computer," I said. "He bonked but I didn't."

"It takes about thirty seconds for SCIC to set in," my dad said. "At this point, we know that the bull animation plus the subliminals can trigger a coma, but we still don't know how. Or why."

"Seventy-two percent," said Gilly.

We all looked at him.

"You said seventy-two percent of people were affected."

"That's right," said my father.

"But one hundred percent of your test subjects succumbed."

"Yes."

"Elf sounds," said the Sasquatch.

"Elf sounds?" I said.

"Seventy-two out of one hundred Flinkwater residents use D-Monix computers. Did you use D-Monix tabs for your tests?"

My father nodded slowly. We stared at Gilly as

he stirred another spoonful of honey into his tea.

"What do elves have to do with it?" I asked.

"E-L-F, stands for Extremely Low Frequency," my dad said. "Infrasonics. Sounds below what the human ear is capable of hearing. Elephants and whales use it to communicate over long distances."

"Like a supersubwoofer?"

"Precisely," said Gilly.

"Why would they use speakers nobody can hear?" I asked.

"D-Monix claims that their infrasonic-enabled speakers enhance the listening experience on a subliminal level."

"Subliminal," said my father thoughtfully.

"Subliminal," said Gilly. They looked at each other.

"That would explain why I wasn't affected," my mother said. "I use a Google tablet." My mom could be embarrassingly retro.

"Do you mean the Brazen Bull didn't have anything to do with everybody bonking?" I said.

Gilly shook his head. His hair kept on moving after he stopped.

"I suspect that the coma-causing infrasonics were already in the computers. The bull screenie, combined with the subliminals embedded by this boy Billy, acted as a trigger. Though how or why, I do not know. I cannot believe it was an accident."

"I bet Billy could figure it out," I said.

"Billy George—is it possible that he is behind this?"

"No!" I thought for a moment. "Well, it's *possible*. But he would have told me. And he wouldn't have tried to bonk the whole town. I mean, he was the one who figured out how to use the Projac to wake everybody up."

"And he says he knows how to get a bomb through airport security?"

I kept on nodding.

"I would like to meet this boy," Gilly said.

43

"Is This Going to Hurt?"

Once Gilly got hold of an idea, there was no let-ting go—and I'm not talking about the infra-sonics thing, I'm talking about him wanting to meet Billy. He wanted to go right then and there.

"Er . . . ," my dad said.

"What?" said Gilly.

"Ummmm . . . ," said my mother.

I knew what they were thinking, because I was thinking the same thing. Gilly might be one of the most brilliant and powerful people on the planet, but he looked like a . . . well, a *Sasquatch*.

My dad cleared his throat. "You know the DHS has been combing the park in search of the Flinkwater Sasquatch, right? Don't you think they might find your present appearance somewhat . . . alarming?"

"Royce is right, Gilly," my mother added. "It

might be best if we get you cleaned up a bit so they don't shoot first and ask questions later."

Gilly considered her proposal. "Is this going to hurt?"

"Not a bit," said my mother.

Mom sent me on an emergency run over to Aunt Janet's to pick up a suit. My uncle Vaughn was about Gilly's size. It was awkward, because Janet had about a million questions, and I had been sworn to silence. Also, Kellan wanted to kiss me over and over again. I had taught him a new skill. Frankly, it was a little sloppy. But after several messy kisses and lots of unanswerable questions from my aunt, I was soon unicycling my way back home with the suit ... when I was cut off by a black SUV containing you-know-who.

"Good afternoon, Mr. Ffelps," I said.

"Hello, Ginger," said Agent Ffelps, leaning out of the passenger-side window. "We've been looking for you."

"Whyever for?" I inquired as I balanced on the WheelBot.

"What do you have in the bag?" he asked.

"That would be a suit," I said. The bag was clear plastic, and the suitiness of its contents was obvious. "I'm taking it to the dry cleaner's."

"I see," said Agent Ffelps, giving the suit the fish eye. "And what dry cleaner would that be?"

"Milgrim's," I said, naming the only dry cleaner in town.

"On Main Street?" he asked.

I nodded.

"Then why are you proceeding south on Water Street?"

He had me there. I thought quickly.

"Oops," I said.

Ffelps smiled as if he had scored a point. Which he had.

"Ginger, I was wondering if you could tell me what you were doing at the airport this morning."

I stared back at him.

"Ginger?"

"What?"

"I asked you a question."

"Actually, you didn't. You said you were wondering if I could tell you what I was doing at the airport this morning. That is not a question; it is a statement."

I detected a slight reddening of his neck.

"What were you doing at the airport?" he said, keeping his voice level.

"I was meeting somebody."

"Who?"

"Professor Little's fiancée."

"Professor Little—the nanotech expert?"

"Yes."

"I have seen the surveillance videos, Ginger," Ffelps said with a slather of faux patience, "and I am acquainted with Professor Little. He was not present at the airport."

"He looks a little different now. No moles."

Ffelps took a moment to absorb that, blinking like a very slow computer trying to process the sum of two plus two. Unable to reach a solution, he decided to change the subject. Sort of.

"What was Billy George doing there? Besides making bomb threats."

"Billy was not making bomb threats. He was simply pointing out a gap in airport security. Have a nice day, Mr. Ffelps. I have to get to the dry cleaner." I performed a perfect U-turn and set off down the sidewalk at the WheelBot's maximum speed of fifteen miles per hour. The SUV cruised along beside me, its tinted windows rolled up.

I was trying to be cool, but the fact was, I was pretty nervous. Agent Ffelps was kind of a moron, but black SUVs are scary. I rolled down Water Street toward downtown Flinkwater and Milgrim's Cleaners, the SUV never more than twenty feet away. I could have ditched them anytime I wanted—but then they would just drive over to my house and intercept me. What I had to do was ditch them without them knowing they'd been ditched.

Fortunately, I had a plan.

44

The Milgrim Maneuver

Mrs. Milgrim, who ran Milgrim's Cleaners, was a harried, frantic woman for whom every aspect of life was a dire emergency. On several occasions I had helped her out, folding sweaters and bagging suits and dresses. When I walked in carrying the suit, she looked up and said, "Oh dear, I hope you don't need that tomorrow!"

"Actually," I said, "I don't need it at all."

She cocked her head. "At all?"

"I mean, it's clean."

"Oh!" she said, as if she had never heard of such a thing.

"I just thought you might need a little help out back," I said.

"Ginger, you are an angel!" she said. "I have an order for Mr. George that he'll be picking up this afternoon, and I'm way behind."

I could imagine that being late with an order for George G. George might be a problem. The man was fanatical about his suits.

"I don't suppose you could iron a couple of shirts?" she said.

"Absolutely. Just give me a minute." I ran back outside, where the SUV was idling at the curb. Agent Ffelps lowered his window and raised his eyebrows.

"I just wanted to let you know that I'll be a while," I said. "Mrs. Milgrim needs my help. I was wondering if you could keep an eye on my WheelBot?" Suppressing every visible trace of sarcasm, I added, "Crime is rampant in downtown Flinkwater, you know."

I think Agent Ffelps was a little bit suspicious, but he nodded.

In the back room, Mrs. Milgrim was pressing a pair of trousers.

"I'm really really *really* sorry, Mrs. Milgrim, but I just remembered something I have to do. I'll come back and help you another time. Would that be okay?"

Her shoulders sagged. "Of course, dear."

I felt terrible about disappointing her, but I figured I could make it up to her later. I grabbed the suit and ran out the back door into the alley. As I have mentioned before, when it comes to the back alleys of Flinkwater, the DHS is no match for Ginger Crump.

Several backyard and alley shortcuts later, I arrived home to find a tall, thin, clean-shaven, deep-eyed man wearing a pair of my dad's boxer shorts sitting at the kitchen table typing rapidly on a tablet. He looked just like pictures I'd seen of Gilbert Bates before he had disappeared. Except in the pictures he wasn't almost naked.

He looked up when I entered the room.

"The Sasquatch has left the building," he said.

The suit fit. Almost. It was a little short in the arms and legs, but Gilly looked quite elegant, I thought.

"You know, if you'd kept some of that beard, you'd look a little bit like Abe Lincoln," I told him.

Gilly smiled. "Perhaps that will make it easier for me to emancipate the population of Flinkwater."

My dad, who was looking out the front window, said, "Did anybody see you, Ginger?"

"I did run into Agent Ffelps," I said. "But I left him at the dry cleaner's."

My dad looked at me and raised his eyebrows.

"He thinks I'm in the back helping Mrs. Milgrim," I said.

"Good. Though I'm sure he'll show up here eventually." He looked at Gilly. "Gil? Ready for your triumphant return?"

"I am," said Gilly. "First order of business, we get young Billy released and find out exactly how he opened this Pandora's box."

"That may not be so easy."

The doorbell rang. My mom went over to the window and peeked past the curtains.

"Who is it?" my dad asked.

"You're not going to believe this," she said, and opened the door.

It was Billy George.

45

A Matter of National Security

The first meeting of Gilbert Bates and Billy George reminded me of two strange dogs checking each other out. Not that they were sniffing each other's butts or anything, but there was a lot of virtual tail wagging going on.

Billy, of course, was completely awestruck. Gilbert Bates was one of his all-time heroes. And Gilly seemed equally impressed to meet the boy who had, intentionally or not, bonked half of Flinkwater.

Gilly spoke first. "You're the little fellow who started this great rumpus."

Billy said, "Did you really hack the CIA when you were my age?"

"Yes. How did you calibrate the infrasonics for your bull animation?"

"Infrasonics? Cool. But that wasn't me. Did

you really develop the kinesthetic protocols for the first DustBot on a three-gig laptop?"

"Two-gig handheld. How did you determine the temporal parameters for your visual subliminals?"

"I used a D-Monix randomizer program and a retinal analyzer. It was easy."

"As I suspected. The bull animation and the visual subliminals are spurious. The OS must have overlaid the infrasonic track based on your program's frequency of deployment."

I wasn't sure if they were attempting to communicate, or just throwing big words around to impress each other.

I tried to coax them back into the real world. "Billy, how did you get them to let you go?"

Billy blinked and turned his head toward me as if he had forgotten I was there, which he probably had. "They didn't let me go, exactly. I just sort of walked out."

We all stared at him.

"You walked out of a TSA holding facility?" my dad asked.

"The lock on my cell sort of popped open."

"Popped open?" my dad said.

"Well, I was kind of fiddling with it. Their security isn't actually all that good."

My dad made one of his deep frowns. "This is not good," he said.

"I know," Billy said. "I could show them how to make their locks better."

"I mean, it's not good because they're going to be looking for you. I'm afraid your escape will only convince them that you're a dangerous criminal."

"What kind of lock was it?" Gilly asked.

"A Yale-Kalichnikov Model Five Thousand."

Gilly looked impressed. "That is a very good lock!"

"Not *that* good," Billy said.

The doorbell rang. My mom ran to the window.

"They're back," she said.

My dad jumped to his feet. "Ginger, Billy, into the safe room."

"You have a safe room?" Billy said. "Cool!"

The agents knocked on the door in a very not-nice way.

"Quickly!" my dad said.

Back when I was a toddler, my father built a secret room between the living room and the kitchen. You would never know it was there unless you measured every room in the house. He claimed it was in case of zombie attack, but knowing my dad, I think it was really because ever since he was a kid he'd wanted to live in a house with a secret room.

Naturally, we ended up using it to store stuff that wouldn't fit in our closets.

I pulled open the concealed door at the back of the pantry and stepped inside.

"Come on," I said to Billy.

"It's kind of small," he said, looking inside.

It *was* kind of small—only about four feet wide and seven feet long, and crowded with boxes, piles of old clothing, and an old exercise bike.

Billy immediately climbed onto the exercise bike. The seat was too high for his feet to reach the pedals.

"Be careful," I said. "It's tippy."

I closed the door. It was dark.

"It's dark," Billy said.

"Just a second." I felt around and slid aside a panel. Light flooded into the small space. We were looking into the living room through a pane of glass. "They can't see us," I said. "It's one-way glass. From the other side it looks like a mirror."

"Cool!" He leaned toward the glass and the exercise bike started to tilt. I grabbed the handlebar.

"Be careful!" I whispered. "You'll bust right through the glass!"

My mom was moving toward the front door to answer it when suddenly it burst open and four men wearing face shields and SWAT gear came charging into the room waving handguns and screaming at everybody to get down on the floor and put their hands behind their heads.

My mom and dad did what they asked, but Gilly just stood there in his suit looking confused. One of the men shot him with a stun gun. Gilly collapsed. The man with the stun gun raised his face shield.

It was Agent Ffelps.

"Can we hear what they're saying?" Billy said.

I fumbled around and quietly slid open the air vent under the mirror.

"—where is your daughter?" Agent Ffelps was shouting.

"We don't know," my dad said. I think that might have been the first time I ever heard him lie. I was so proud.

As Agent Ffelps directed his minions to search the house, I noticed my mother giving him her most chilling glare.

"Agent Ffelps," she said, her voice cracking like a bullwhip.

He pointed his gun at her and smiled. Smarmily. My mother was unimpressed.

"You. Broke. My. Front. Door." Each word reduced the curvature of Ffelps's smile by a couple of millimeters. Mom can have that effect on people.

He said, "Mrs. Crump, your daughter and her friend Billy George are in serious trouble."

"At least they do not go around breaking people's doors down," she said.

"This is a matter of national security." He gestured with his gun at Gilly. "And who might *this* be?"

Gilly groaned and tried to sit up.

"That," said my father, "is Gilbert Bates."

46

An Arresting Development

"Agent Ffelps," said my mother.

Ffelps ignored her—never a good idea. His attention was on Gilly.

"Agent *Ffelps*!" My mother's voice got Ffelps's attention.

"Yes?" he said with feigned mildness.

My mother, in full witch-queen mode, got right in his face. "That door *will* be repaired within the hour, accompanied by an apology from you and your superiors. And I will see to it that it comes out of your personal paycheck." She stabbed his chest with a red-nailed forefinger. "Your *last* paycheck, I might add."

Ffelps's face turned a few shades paler, but he held on to his smile.

"Mrs. Crump, that door is the least of your concerns right now."

"Perhaps, but it is the greatest of *your* concerns." She was leaning into him, forcing the agent to bend backward. He wasn't smiling anymore.

"I do not work for you, Mrs. Crump."

"That goes without saying—as if I would ever hire an incompetent fool of your limited intellect and capabilities. Breaking people's doors down. Where did you get your social skills? Klingon language camp?"

Ffelps blinked confusedly. My mother's clever Star Trek reference went so far over his head it might as well have been on Deep Space Nine.

The men with guns were returning from their search of the house, shaking their heads.

"Please control yourself, Mrs. Crump," Ffelps said. "You're getting hysterical."

"*Hysterical?*" Her eyes blazed, and both my dad and Gilly jumped forward and grabbed her arms before she could rake her claws down Agent Ffelps's face.

"Cuff her!" Ffelps shouted. "You're under arrest!"

The DHS agents may have been incompetent fools, but they were very good at handcuffing. Within seconds my mother was in shackles, and Agent Ffelps had recovered his smarmy smile.

"That's better," he said. He turned to Gilly. "You are Gilbert Bates?"

"I am," said Gilly.

"I thought you were dead."

"Do I look dead?"

"Not entirely," Agent Ffelps admitted.

Gilly said, "May I ask what the lady is being charged with?"

"I would be interested to know that as well," said my father.

"National security," Ffelps snapped.

"You are charging her with national security?" my father said.

"I mean, it is a *matter* of national security."

Gilly interrupted them. "Agent Ffelps, it is imperative that I speak with a young man you have in your custody," Gilly said.

"And what young man would that be?"

"Billy George."

Agent Ffelps looked startled. It was a brilliant move on Gilly's part. By demanding to see Billy, he had deflected any suspicion that he might know where Billy was.

"What do you want with the boy?" Ffelps asked

"I believe he may be the key to solving the mystery of the SCIC outbreak."

"We already know that. In fact, Billy George is now a fugitive. I thought we might find him here."

"Here?" Gilly managed to look surprised.

Agent Ffelps nodded. "We believe that the girl"—he looked at my mother—"your smart-mouthed daughter—may have helped him escape from our holding facility."

I decided it was time for me to make an appearance.

"Stay here," I said to Billy as I slipped out the back entrance of the secret room and sauntered down the hallway to join them. Putting on my best flabbergasted expression, I said, "Agent Ffelps? What are *you* doing here?"

Agent Ffelps looked at me, startled.

"Where did *you* come from?"

I gave him a haughty look. "When scary men with guns burst into our house, I hide. Under my bed."

Ffelps glowered at his men.

"We *checked* under the bed," one of the men insisted.

"You must have mistaken me for a dust bunny," I said. "Why is my mom in handcuffs?"

"She assaulted a federal agent," said Ffelps.

"I assaulted no one," my mom said, assaulting Ffelps with her eyes.

"That is true," said Gilly.

My father nodded in agreement. "I saw no assault."

Ffelps knew he had a problem. My mother's nonassault had been witnessed by the most famous and wealthy former missing person in the world, and the director of ACPOD cyber security. But I could tell he was afraid to uncuff her. The way she was looking at him I couldn't blame him.

My father said, "Amanda, if Agent Ffelps removes your handcuffs, will you promise not to claw his eyes out?"

"Only if he agrees to fix my door. Today!"

Ffelps sagged. "All right. I will see that your door is repaired. Uncuff her."

A moment later my mother was free, and you never saw such a roomful of tense-looking men. Keeping a nervous eye on her, Ffelps turned to me.

"Ginger," he said.

"Agent Ffelps," I replied.

"Your young friend Billy George escaped from DHS custody. We would like to know how that was accomplished, and where he is now."

"How would *I* know?" I sneaked a glance at the one-way mirror and winked.

"Agent Ffelps," my dad said in his most reasonable voice, "are you actually suggesting that my thirteen-year-old daughter broke a prisoner out of a high-security DHS holding cell?"

"I admit it seems unlikely," said Ffelps, "but I cannot believe that little boy walked out on his own."

A sudden loud thump came from the wall, and a long crack appeared in the mirror. We all jumped back as the mirror exploded outward, followed by Billy George, his legs tangled in the frame of the tippy exercise bike.

Ffelps's eyes bulged.

"Arrest them all!" he shouted.

Episode Five

The Flinkwater Factor

47

Jailed

The DHS holding facility was a prefab plasticized-concrete block house—a single open space with three small cells along one wall. They put me in the middle cell with Billy. My parents were in the cell to our left, and Gilly was on the other side of us.

Mom was in a really bad mood.

"They left our front door wide open." She kept repeating that over and over. "We could be robbed."

"Mom, nobody steals anything in Flinkwater."

That earned me a glare. "Just last week, Mavis Dunhill's wheelbarrow was stolen."

"J.G. took it," Billy said. He was untying his shoelace.

"I thought J.G. was reformed," I said.

"He's gone into the food business," Billy said.

"He buys pizzas and burritos and delivers them to the DHS guys. That's what the wheelbarrow was for. Those DHS guys love him."

"They don't know him," I said.

Billy pulled the shoelace from his sneaker and looked at Gilly, who was gnawing on his thumbnail.

"Yale-Kalichnikov Model Five Thousand," Billy said. "You ready?"

Gilly said, "Go!"

Agent Ffelps was no mental giant, and he clearly had no understanding of the Flinkwater Factor.

What is the Flinkwater Factor, you ask?

The Flinkwater Factor was one of Gilbert Bates's most brilliant ideas. When you put a large number of Very Smart, Very Geeky persons in a confined space where there is nothing to do but compete with one another, remarkable things are bound to happen. That was the main reason he'd put ACPOD in the tiny town of Flinkwater, Iowa.

Something similar happened in Silicon Valley back in the 1900s. In fact, many of the ACPOD engineers had been born out there. But it was in Flinkwater that the geeky-techie concentration reached critical mass. Gilbert Bates had dubbed it the Flinkwater Factor and claimed it was the reason for ACPOD's remarkable success.

Putting the two geekiest, smartest hackers on

the planet in adjacent cells was like a miniature version of the Flinkwater Factor.

Billy, using the hard plastic tip of his shoelace, opened our cell door in three minutes flat. Gilly used a paring from his thumbnail to pop his open a few seconds later.

They gave each other a high five, then quickly dashed back to their cells when we heard the sound of the outer door opening. A moment later Agent Ffelps entered the holding area, followed by the handsomest man in the world.

You know, of course, who I'm talking about.

48

The Uncanny Josh Stevens

People can disagree about who is or isn't handsome. But most people would put Josh Stevens at the top of their list.

According to his official bio, Josh Stevens was one quarter Korean, one quarter Irish, one eighth Ethiopian, one eighth Native American, one eighth Norwegian, and one eighth Basque. If all that were true, he had inherited all the best-looking features from each of his ancestors.

Allow me to describe him. Classic, chiseled features with a slightly arced nose, glittering hazel eyes with a hint of epicanthic fold from his half-Korean grandmother, flawless skin of burnished bronze, thick black hair with a few nicely placed auburn strands, and a smile showing the optimum number of toothpaste-ad-perfect teeth. He was impeccably dressed, as always, in a perfectly fitted suit, his jacket casually unbuttoned to show off his trademark black silk collarless shirt.

A few years ago a rumor that Josh Stevens was actually a computer simulation went viral. I have to admit, I almost believed it. He was just so perfect-looking, it was hard to believe he was real. I figured that the photos and broadcasts had to be tweaked, the same way Professor Little and Hillary had made themselves look mole free when they chatted online.

Which was why I was amazed to discover that in person he looked *exactly* like his virtual image. Unbelievably handsome.

But at the same time he was even more repulsive than Professor Little, pre-mole-removal. He looked like a refugee from the Uncanny Valley.

The only thing creepier than a robot that looks almost exactly like a human is a human that looks like an uncannily handsome and human-looking robot. Nobody likes people who have no flaws, and except for being flawless, Josh Stevens was as flaw free as it is possible for a person to be. In other words, he was really creepy—and never more creepy than when he bestowed his five-hundred-watt smile upon us all. His glittering hazel eyes flickered across me and Billy, instantly dismissing us. The eyes paused a fraction of a second on my dad, and a bit longer on my mother, then moved to Gilly. Target acquired. The five-hundred-watt smile jumped to one thousand watts.

"Gilbert!" he exclaimed.

Gilly, his long fingers wrapped around the bars of his cell, glared at Stevens.

"Josh. I am surprised."

"Surprised?" said Stevens. *"Pourquoi?"* That means "why" in French.

"Parce que I detect a hair out of place," said Gilly, countering Stevens's pretentious French with sarcastic French.

Stevens's right hand jerked toward his perfectly tousled hair. He caught himself, threw his head back, and laughed. A little too loudly, I thought.

"Same old Gil," he said. He looked around the facility as if seeing it for the first time. "How are they treating you here?"

"As well as can be expected. We will not be staying long."

"Really! That's not what I heard. In fact, the Department of Homeland Security recently informed me that you have been involved in terrorist activities. I was quite surprised, of course. Ffelps here seems to think they will need to hold you indefinitely."

Ffelps nodded grimly.

"In the meantime, the DHS has asked me to take over the reins at ACPOD."

Gilly's eyes bulged slightly and his knuckles whitened. I half expected him to throw open the cell door and strangle Stevens, but he kept his cool.

"George George might have something to say about that," Gilly said.

"George is fine with it," Stevens said. "He and I have become quite close over the past several months."

"Why would George G. George want anything to do with *you*?" I blurted.

Josh Stevens looked at me as if I were a piece of furniture that had suddenly spoken.

"Who are you?" he asked.

"Your worst nightmare." I'd been waiting my whole life to say that.

"Well, your *hair* certainly fits that description." He turned back to Gilly. "George realized that he needed some help, especially after the SCIC event. Clearly, ACPOD is not capable of handling its own security. I proposed a friendly takeover, and of course the DHS was delighted that D-Monix could be of assistance. Isn't that right, Agent Ffelps?"

Ffelps nodded. Meanwhile, I was about to explode. I think it was his remark about my hair. I could see that my dad was reaching critical pressure as well, since he was supposed to be in charge of ACPOD security.

Gilly said, "This is highly illegal. I will not let you get away with it."

"Illegal?" Stevens chuckled. "Flinkwater is under martial law, which means that the government can do whatever it pleases. I am simply performing my role as a patriot. You, on the other hand, are a terrorist and a Sasquatch, and have no legal rights whatsoever."

"I am not a terrorist."

"Ah, but you are! For one thing, you have been lurking about in the woods for months and making visits to the ACPOD laboratories for unknown purposes. We have video." He looked at my father. "I'm really surprised at you, Royce. We know you had access to that surveillance footage. You should have reported a Sasquatch breaking through ACPOD security."

"You're saying I should have reported that the majority shareholder and chairman of ACPOD entered his own facilities?" my dad said.

"I was just keeping an eye on things," Gilly muttered.

"The DHS disagrees," Stevens said. "And you are a known associate of a known terrorist who stole a working prototype of a Projac and engineered the SCIC outbreak." He smirked at Billy, who was staring at him openmouthed. "Furthermore, another of your associates was heard to threaten DHS officers with bodily harm." He looked at my mother. "You're fired, by the way."

My mother attempted to kill him with her eyes. Alas, she failed.

"As for curly top here," he said, showing me his perfect teeth, "she is suspected of abducting a valuable experimental animal."

"Mr. Stevens," my father said, his voice carefully controlled, "all of your allegations are unproven and, in fact, dead wrong—"

Not *entirely* wrong, I thought.

"—and you have no right to keep us here. I demand to speak with George G. George. This is all a simple misunderstanding. I'm sure we can quickly clear things up."

Josh Stevens hit him with his megawatt smile. "You're fired too. In a few hours, you will all be transferred to a high-security federal facility in Des Moines. Until then, you folks will just have to make yourselves comfortable. And rest assured, ACPOD is in good hands."

With his gloating session complete, the handsomest and most repulsive man in the world left the room, followed by the smarmily smiling Agent Ffelps.

49

Jailbreak

For several seconds after Stevens and Ffelps left, none of us spoke. I could hear the faint whistle of my mother breathing through her nose, like a bull preparing to charge.

Finally, Gilly said, "Well, *that* was unpleasant."

"I will pull out his teeth one by one and make him swallow them," my mother said—a rather shocking statement, even from my mom.

"If they put us in a federal prison we might be there a long time," my father said.

Gilly and Billy pushed open their unlocked cell doors. While Billy opened my dad's cell, Gilly went to the outer door and looked through the tiny window.

"There are three guards," he said.

As much as I liked being out of my cell, I didn't see what good it would do us. Even if we somehow made it past the guards and escaped, we would be fugitives, Flinkwater would still be under martial law, and ACPOD would remain at the mercy of Josh Stevens. I pointed this out to Gilly.

"Freedom is the first step to enlightenment," he said cryptically.

Billy examined the outer door. "This one won't be so easy," he said. "It's not keyed from the inside, and I don't see how we can slip the bolt."

"It hardly matters," said my father. "Even if we could get it open, there are three men outside with guns."

"Only two now," said Gilly, who was peering out the window. "One of them just ran off. He seemed to be in a hurry."

"Still, two is two too many."

"They're arguing about something," Gilly said. "Now another one has run off. He's sort of bent over, like he has a stomachache. And the other one looks rather ill. Oh—there he goes too! They're all gone."

"Can you see where they went?"

Gilly stepped back from the door. "Judging from the way they were moving, I'd say they're headed for the latrine."

The latch clicked. Billy jumped back. The door swung slowly open.

"Good job," Gilly said.

"It wasn't me," said Billy.

The door opened all the way and the last person on earth I expected to see stepped into the room.

50

Fast Food

You remember Johnston George, aka J.G.? Billy's psychotic older brother? Who later became the most popular kid at Flinkwater High? Yes?

Well, it was J.G. who opened that door.

We all just stood there, stunned.

"Who are you?" Gilly asked after a few seconds.

"That's my brother," Billy said. "Approach with extreme caution."

"We'd better get going," J.G. said. "I don't know how long it'll be before those guys are done."

"Done what?" I asked. "Where did they go?"

"I put a little Ultra-Lax in their lunch burritos," J.G. said.

"They took off in quite a rush," my mother observed. "How much laxative did you use?"

"I guess about twelve capsules."

"*Twelve* laxative pills for *three* guards?"

"No. Twelve for each burrito."

"Oh."

"We gotta go," J.G. said, heading out the door. "Come on!"

Considering that the DHS has more than three million employees and is one of the most powerful institutions in the government, their security was rather *lax*. Pun intended. J.G. led us around the back of the holding facility to a twelve-foot-tall high-voltage chain-link fence topped with an endless loop of deadly-looking razor wire.

"How are we supposed to get through *that*?" I asked.

J.G. laughed and pointed at a weathered sheet of plywood lying on the ground next to the fence. He dragged the plywood aside to reveal a hole about four feet deep. The hole led to a tunnel under the fence. I noticed another sheet of plywood on the other side. Mavis Dunhill's stolen wheelbarrow was parked nearby.

"You dug this just to get us out?" I said, impressed.

"Nah, I've been going in and out of here a lot doing my food runs. Those DHS guys, they tip real good."

"Why don't you just bring the food in through the gate?"

J.G. looked at me as if I were the psychotic one.

"What fun would that be? Besides, this is faster, and I don't have to answer a bunch of questions." He climbed into the tunnel, followed by Billy and Gilly. "Last person through has to pull the board back over the hole," he called back.

My mother was looking into the hole askance. "I am not crawling through the dirt," she said.

"Well *I* am," I said, and jumped into the hole after Gilly. As I made my way under the fence I heard my father say, "Honey, if you want a shot at Agent Ffelps, you're going to have to get dirty."

Moments later we had all made it to a small wooded area outside the compound. My mother was brushing frantically at the soiled and shredded knees of her tights with one hand and holding her high-heeled shoes in the other.

51

Set to Kill

Getting out of the compound was easy compared to figuring out what to do next. Mom wanted to go straight to Agent Ffelps and give him a piece of her mind, but of course that would just have gotten her thrown back in a cage. Dad wanted to send me and Billy to Florida to stay with Uncle Ashton, but there was no way we'd make it through airport security. Gilly wanted to break into the ACPOD research center where he hoped to discover the details of Josh Stevens's nefarious plan.

As for J.G., he wanted to go home and take Billy with him. To no one's surprise, J.G. hadn't sprung us out of the goodness of his shriveled black heart. He had ulterior motives.

"I can't work my tablet," J.G. said. "Something's screwy with it. I need Billy to fix it."

"You broke us out of jail so that Billy could

help you with a computer problem?" my mother
said, incredulous.

J.G. shrugged. "He knows how to fix stuff."

"Did you try turning it on?" Billy said.

J.G. thought for a moment. "Yeah, I did. A
bunch of times."

"And what happened?"

"Nothing."

"Nothing?"

"Well, it sort of belched."

Billy nodded as if belching tablets were perfectly common. None of *my* tabs, I want you to
know, have ever belched.

"What did you do to it?" Billy asked, giving his
brother a suspicious look.

"Nothing much . . . well . . . I was shooting at a
fly this morning, and it landed on my tablet."

"Shooting at a fly? With what?"

J.G. hesitated, then said, "A Projac."

"You have *another* Projac?"

"I sort of borrowed it from Dad. After the first
Projac got swiped from the lab, he brought a second prototype home for safekeeping, and . . ." J.G.
grinned and shrugged. "There was this fly."

"Where is this Projac now?" I asked.

J.G. reached under his shirt and came out with
the Projac. I grabbed it.

"Hey!"

I pointed the Projac at his face. That shut him up fast. He started backing away.

"Ginger, honey," my father said in a shaky voice as he reached for the weapon. He looked scared. I handed him the Projac. He made an adjustment to a small slide control on the handle. "This is a Military Model PJ-297," he said. "It was set to kill."

J.G., white-faced, had put about ten yards between us. He turned and ran.

"I wasn't going to shoot him," I said in a small voice. I was lying. I had almost pulled the trigger.

My father put the Projac in his pocket. "We can't go to our house—it's the first place they'll look. And we can't go to J.G. and Billy's home. Gilly's right. Our only hope is to break into the ACPOD labs and try to find some evidence that will clear us. The question is, how do we get in without being caught?"

"I know a way," I said.

The ACPOD campus was only a quarter of a mile away, but it felt like longer—especially to my mom, who was attempting to walk through the woods in her high heels. After falling down a couple of times, she hung her heels on a tree branch and continued in her stockinged feet, complaining all the way. The five of us eventually reached the edge of the trees just behind Area 51, the animal research building.

"Myke Duchakis told me he hacked the lock on the south door," I said. "We should be able to walk right in."

"What about the cameras and motion sensors?" my dad asked.

"Myke said they've been disabled. At least they were a week ago."

"If I ever get my job back I'm going to beef up security." He looked at Gilly. "You ready?"

Gilly nodded, and the two of them left the cover of the trees and headed for the door. I started to follow, but Dad turned back and said, "Ginger, you wait here with Billy and your mom."

A few seconds after my dad and Gilly entered the building, Billy said, "Forget that! I'm going in." He ran toward the door and disappeared inside.

"I'm going in too," I said. I looked at my mother.

"Well, I'm certainly not standing around out here by myself," she said with a grim set to her jaw.

52

Area 51

Inside we found the saddest collection of animals you could imagine. Monkeys, dogs, rats, and even a raccoon, each confined to their own cage, many of them with odd-looking devices attached to their bodies. We caught up with Gilly, my dad, and Billy in the dog section. They were standing in front of a standard poodle who was wearing a collar similar to the one Redge had been wearing.

My dad saw us coming and said, "Of course, I never *really* thought you would follow my instructions."

I read the sign on the poodle's cage. "'Subject TX9301,'" I read. "That's a terrible name," I said to the morose-looking poodle.

The poodle yipped piteously.

"*My name is Kill Bark Kill,*" said the poodle's collar.

"Much better," I said. "I'd like to put that collar on Agent Ffelps and see how *he* likes it."

"I like the way you think," said Gilly. He looked from me to Billy and raised one eyebrow. Billy laughed, then reached though the bars of the poodle's cage, removed the collar, and gently detached the leads cemented to the dog's partially shaven skull. He put the collar in his pocket and continued down the row of animals. Billy, Gilly, and my dad led the way, discussing something in low voices.

"How come there's nobody here?" I asked.

"It's Sunday," my mom said. "Most of our employees take the day off."

We proceeded through the building until we reached the main entrance. A single guard was sitting slumped at his desk, snoring. My dad checked the setting on the Projac and shot him. The only difference was that the guard began snoring a bit louder.

"When I get my job back, this one's fired," my dad said, pocketing the Projac. He lifted the unconscious guard from his chair and laid him out on the floor.

"I think he's closest to your size," Gilly said to my dad.

Gilly took a seat at the guard's terminal and began typing rapidly as my father removed the guard's shirt and cap.

"What are we doing?" I asked Billy.

Billy grinned and said, "Baiting a trap,"

"Trap for who?"

"You'll see."

My dad took off his shirt and donned the guard's blue uniform shirt and cap. He and Billy then dragged the guard back down the hall and locked him in one of the empty dog cages. When they returned, Gilly had finished whatever it was he'd been typing.

"He'll be here shortly," he said.

My father took a seat at the guard station, while the rest of us retreated back down the hallway and waited. A few minutes later we heard the front door buzz, and a familiar voice.

"Well? You said you had some information for me?"

I peeked around the corner. Agent Ffelps, hands on his hips, was standing before the guard desk, looking rather impatient.

"Actually," my father said, "I'm afraid it's you who have information for me."

He raised the Projac, smiled, and shot Ffelps in the chest.

53

Franklin Foster Ffelps

"Please state your full name," my father said.

Agent Ffelps pressed his lips together, but the speaker on the collar around his neck spoke: *"Franklin Foster Ffelps."*

Ffelps's eyes widened. Billy, who was sitting beside my father, grinned.

"I told you it would work," he said. "The Collar of Truth never lies."

The three of them were sitting in one of the observation rooms used by the animal researchers. Ffelps was tied to a chair, and not at all happy about it. Gilly, my mom, and I were in the next room, observing them through a one-way-glass window.

"And what is your relationship with Josh Stevens?" my father asked.

Ffelps gritted his teeth, his jaw muscle

bunching. But the Collar of Truth spoke.

"I do whatever he tells me."

"And why is that? I thought you worked for the Department of Homeland Security."

"I do!" Ffelps said.

"Stevens pays me," said the collar.

"No!" said Ffelps.

"Yes!" said the dog collar.

"Agent Ffelps, you cannot lie to me. No matter what you say, the collar will transmit your true thoughts."

By this time Ffelps was turning bright red, his cheek was twitching, and his eyes had a teary glaze. "Take it off!" he cried.

"Who gave Stevens access to the ACPOD protocols and mainframes?"

"Please—take this blasted thing off me!"

"There's no way out of this," said the dog collar. *"I'm trapped!"*

"I'll tell you everything!" Ffelps wailed.

The collar continued to speak: *"They know everything. My career is over. I'll be in prison for the rest of my life. What have I done? I'm ruined. I'll never—"*

My father flipped a switch on the collar. The speaker fell silent.

"It was George George," Ffelps said.

In the next room Gilly set down the microphone

into which he had been speaking and smiled.

"Good job," said my mother. "You could have a second career as a mind reader."

"Just a few educated guesses about what the man was really thinking," he said modestly.

"George George was behind the SCIC outbreak?" my father asked Ffelps.

Ffelps, utterly defeated, said, "No, that was Stevens. George just went along with it. Stevens rigged every tablet D-Monix shipped to Flinkwater with a coma-inducing infrasonic program embedded in that ridiculous Brazen Bull screen saver."

"Not screen saver," I whispered to myself. "*Screenie.*"

"Why use the Brazen Bull?" my father asked. "And what about the subliminals Billy added to the program?"

"That was merely a convenient coincidence. Stevens used the screen saver to hide his ELF program because it was the most commonly used app in Flinkwater. The subliminal images were simply a lucky break—Stevens discovered the boy's little joke and used it as a trigger. That way if it were discovered, Billy George would be blamed. The entire SCIC crisis was a ruse to give the DHS an excuse to come in and take over the town, while giving Stevens total access to ACPOD. He planned to create a new line of cybernetically-controlled animals here, then use the animals to replace ACPOD's robots. He thought it would be amusing to use ACPOD's own research facilities to create a line of robotized animals. He had plans to breed a line of cute little cyberbunnies."

"What for?" I asked.

"Dustbunny two-point-oh," Ffelps said. "A fuzzy little bunny makes for a good dust mop. Stevens is determined to win the Dustbunny/ DustBot war and drive ACPOD out of business."

"But people still won't want a houseful of rabbits," Billy pointed out.

Ffelps shrugged. "I never said it was a *good* idea."

"What did Stevens have on George George?" my dad asked.

Ffelps coughed out a bitter laugh and looked at Billy with an expression that was equal parts amusement and despair. "Have you ever wondered why you don't look anything like your parents?"

54

Unnatural Selection

The story Agent Ffelps told us later became front page news. I'm sure you've read about it. But just in case you've been in a coma for the past several weeks, allow me to explain.

A decade ago, around the time that ACPOD became the largest and most successful robotics, cybernetics, and artificial intelligence company on earth, Gilbert Bates had been happily married to an ACPOD researcher named Jenny Winedot. The couple had one child, a bright, cheerful three-year-old boy named Nigel, who disappeared one day. His disappearance led to the suicide of Jenny Winedot and the depression that had caused Gilbert Bates to abandon the company he had founded.

Until Agent Ffelps told us his story, young Nigel Bates was presumed to have drowned in the Raccoona River.

"This all happened while I was a junior agent for the Iowa branch of the DHS," Agent Ffelps recounted. "Naturally, we kept close tabs on everything that happened in Flinkwater because ACPOD is a Department of Defense contractor. When one of the ACPOD executives and his wife decided to adopt a child, we monitored the process. George G. George was that executive, and the child he adopted was you." Ffelps looked at Billy.

"I'm adopted?" Billy said. "You mean I'm not related to J.G.?"

"I'm afraid not."

"Fantastic!" Billy looked delighted.

"You were formally adopted two months after Nigel Bates disappeared," Ffelps said.

"Are you saying . . . I'm Nigel Bates?"

Ffelps nodded.

"Nigel?" Billy said.

"How can you possibly know this?" my father asked.

Ffelps's mouth curved into a prim, intensely irritating smile. "I know a great deal. George George was the vice president of ACPOD at the time. George has always been an ambitious man, and as long as Gilbert Bates was running ACPOD, George had no opportunity for advancement. For a man like George G. George, that was intolerable.

"George was part of the search party after Nigel's disappearance, and he found the boy, alive and well, sitting on a driftwood log on the bank of the river. Instead of returning Nigel to his parents, George G. George took the boy home and concealed him in his subbasement. I suspect that George simply wanted to punish Gilbert Bates. He probably only planned to hold the boy for a day or two before pretending to find him and making himself a hero. But once he saw how miserable Gilbert and Jenny had become, he decided to keep the boy for a while longer, purely out of spite. Then, when Jenny threw herself into the river and drowned, he saw a new opportunity. If Gilbert Bates, in his grief, was unable to perform his duties at ACPOD, he would have to step down, and George George would be promoted to president.

"So he made private arrangements to adopt a child. Using bogus papers and a crooked adoption service, he adopted Nigel, gave him the name Billy, and the rest you know."

"How is it that no one recognized Nigel?" my father asked.

"They bleached his hair, for one thing." He looked at Billy. "Have you ever wondered why your hair is blond in the photos of you as a toddler?"

"My mom said it got brown later," Billy said.

Ffelps nodded. "Gilbert and Jenny were the

only two people who knew their child well, and they were both gone. By the time you were old enough to go to school, you looked different enough that no one who knew you as a three-year-old suspected your true identity."

"When did you learn about this?" my father asked.

"Oh, I've known it all along. We monitored the adoption, and I saw right away that the boy was the Bates boy."

"And you didn't tell anybody?"

"It wasn't a security issue. Also, I thought it might be a piece of information that would come in handy some day. And it did." He frowned. "Although I must admit that the end result is not what I would have hoped."

"How did Josh Stevens become involved?"

"I'd been doing private work for Stevens for years. Mostly I just let him know what was going on at ACPOD—shipping manifests, movement of executives, presentations to the Pentagon, and so forth. Last year I traded him my information about Nigel Bates in exchange for a boat."

"A boat?" Billy said.

"It is a very nice boat," said Agent Ffelps proudly. "A twenty-nine foot Amberjack with twin diesels. Sleeps two." His face fell. "I suppose now I'll have to sell it to pay my defense lawyer."

"What did Josh Stevens do with that information?"

"He spoke with George G. George, I imagine. A few months later George ordered a special shipment of D-Monix tablets for all the ACPOD engineers and their families. You know the rest."

55

Back to Normal—for Flinkwater, That Is.

The video of that interview, along with a signed confession by Agent Ffelps, went out within the hour to my uncle Ashton, who made sure it was instantly picked up by all the major news organizations. Uncle Ashton is good at things like that. And I'm sure you know what happened next: splash page on all the news sites, congressional hearings, the media circus. There was even a short-lived boycott of D-Monix tablets, but that didn't last. As I've said before, D-Monix tabs rock—even without the infrasonics.

George G. George avoided prison by testifying against Josh Stevens. George was put on probation. He now works on Elwin Hogg's pig farm.

Former DHS agent Franklin Foster Ffelps spent a few months in prison, but was released

on a work program. He is now employed as a jani-
tor for ACPOD and reports directly to my mother,
who has been happily making his life as miserable
as possible.

Josh Stevens fled the country to seek asylum in
Venezuela, where he is now the National Director
of Cyber-security. D-Monix has been taken over by
McDonald's and has shifted its business model to
the production of interactive talking hamburgers—
a big hit with the preschool crowd.

Gilbert Bates was reinstated as the president
and CEO of ACPOD, and of course my parents got
their jobs back.

The DHS, badly embarrassed by the whole
fiasco, has withdrawn from Flinkwater, except for
the TSA agents at the airport, who continue to con-
fiscate dangerous contraband such as baby bottles
and plastic butter knives.

One of the first things Gilly did when he took
back the reins at ACPOD was to dismantle the animal research program and turn the Area 51 building into a free walk-in veterinary and adoption
clinic. Myke volunteers there on weekends.

Professor Little married his fiancée, Hillary,
and opened a mole-removal clinic in St. Petersburg,
Florida, the world capital of unsightly moles.

J.G., after his brief stint as the most popular boy
in Flinkwater, and after "heroically" engineering

the jailbreak that allowed us to defeat the forces of
evil, slipped back into his old ways. While visiting
his father at Elwin Hogg's farm, he was caught in
the act of spray-painting Garganchewous, Elwin's
prize boar, with lime-green and pink graffiti. Elwin
was understandably upset, as he had planned to sell
the enormous pig at a breeders' auction that week.
Instead of letting J.G. off with a stern warning, he
called the FBI and told them he had captured an
agricultural terrorist. J.G. and his mother were
forced to leave town. I hear J.G. is now conducting
his reign of terror in a small town west of Omaha,
Nebraska.

Redge the talking dog became famous when
Gerald Ruff put him online to advertise his roofing
business. The video went viral, and "Ruff! Roof!"
became a catchphrase. Last I heard, Gerald had
hired sixty new employees and was doing roofing
jobs from Dubuque to Council Bluffs.

Dipwad the talking monkey remains at
large and was last seen in the snack aisle at the
Economart tearing into a bag of peanuts and calling the employees "stinky no-tails."

As for Billy, he's moved in with his real dad,
Gilly. But he didn't actually move. Billy did not
wish to give up his subbasement hideaway, so Gilly
bought the house from the Georges and moved in.
Also, Billy insists on keeping the name Billy.

"Who names their kid *Nigel*?" he asked—but he didn't say it in front of his father.

Other than that, our lives returned to what passes for normal in Flinkwater: lots of boring stuff interrupted from time to time by moments of terror.

For example, just last week, on my fourteenth birthday, I walked over to Billy's and found him standing stock still in his backyard. He saw me coming and said, barely moving his mouth, "Do not move."

I did not move.

He rolled his eyes up and to the right. I followed his glance and saw a black, disk-shaped object hovering fifteen feet off the ground.

"Seeker-killer drone," he said through his teeth.

That sounded ominous, to put it mildly. Had Josh Stevens sent a drone assassin all the way from Venezuela to kill us?

"What do we do?" I said, imitating Billy's clenched-jaw speaking style.

The drone rotated, then sank slowly to head height and moved toward me. I stared at it like a deer hypnotized by oncoming headlights. A small tube telescoped from the disk, pointing directly at my face. In that moment I was certain I was about to die, and I had never been kissed.

Billy yelled and jumped up and down, waving

his arms. The drone spun and fired. Billy's chest blossomed blood red; he staggered back and fell.

I screamed. The drone, having successfully performed its task, fell to the ground. I ran to Billy and threw my arms around him, sobbing hysterically as he gasped his final gasp.

Of course, it was not really his final gasp.

"Gin, you're choking me!" he gasped again.

"You're alive!" I exclaimed unnecessarily.

"It's just red paint," he said, sitting up. "I borrowed the drone from the ACPOD test labs and loaded it with mini paintballs."

I punched him on the shoulder, hard.

"Ow! What was that for?"

"For scaring me. I thought you were dead."

"Well, I'm not." He stood up.

"Are you getting taller?" I asked.

He smiled. "A little. I think I'm having a growth spurt."

That was when I kissed him.

There was a moment when I thought I might have made a mistake. Our lips mashed together, and at first it was like all the kissing was happening on my end.

And then he kissed me back.

Science or Fantasy?

The Flinkwater Factor is science fiction. That can mean a story with lots of "sciency" things in it, or a sciency story with lots of fiction. This book has both. Many of the inventions in the book are either real or will be soon. Some are possible but unlikely. And some are flat-out fantasy. Here are a few of them.

Chapter 1 • DustBots

The DustBot is fictional, but it's really just a fancy, semi-intelligent, self-propelled vacuum cleaner—like a smartphone compared to an electric typewriter. Science!

Chapter 3 • Gyroscopic unicycle (WheelBot)

Powered unicycles that hold themselves upright are real. You could buy one today. Science!

Chapter 7 • *Dial phones*

Yes, as ridiculous as it may seem, dial phones are real. They were found in nearly every household as recently as thirty years ago. Retro science!

Chapter 8 • *Subliminal messaging*

Advertisers have experimented with inserting subliminal messages into movies, television, and print ads. Do such messages work? Not very well, according to most studies. Sciency!

Chapter 9 • *Corpus callosum*

The corpus callosum is real—it's a bundle of nerve fibers that connects the left and right halves of the brain. Science!

Chapter 9 • *Positronium gamma-ray laser*

It could be a real thing soon. Science!

Chapter 10 • *Poopnet*

Fantasy! I hope. Nobody wants a stinky Internet connection.

Chapter 11 • *Projac*

Wireless electric stun guns that can operate over a distance are not real—yet. But wait a few more years. Science!

Chapter 11 • *Smart-O-Rang*

Kind of like a futuristic high-tech Nerf ball. I'm sure it will be invented any day now. Science!

Chapter 12 • *The WDK Factor: Do computers ever make mistakes?*

Yes, and no. Errors in computer output can always be traced back to errors in hardware or software construction or design. If your computer tells you that 2+2=5, the answer is wrong, but it's not the computer's fault—somewhere along the line, a human being messed up. Science!

Chapter 13 • *Electroconvulsive therapy*

Electric shock treatments are still used today to help people with serious depression and certain other ailments. Science!

Chapter 16 • *Talking dogs*

As any dog owner knows, dogs do have thoughts, and they do communicate. So do lizards and octopuses. A device that turns a dog's electrical brain activity into human speech is already being developed by a company in Sweden. How well does it work? No idea! Sciency!

Chapter 21 • *Cybernetics*

In 1948 scientist Norbert Wiener defined cybernetics as the "scientific study of control and

communication in the animal and the machine."
Today the term covers a very broad range of scientific
endeavors. Science!

Chapter 21 • *The Uncanny Valley*

Robotics professor Masahiro Mori coined the
term "Uncanny Valley" back in 1970. It describes the
way people react to a robot that looks creepily human.
Science!

Chapter 23 • *Sasquatch*

Tales of hairy, manlike creatures have been told
for thousands of years. In the Himalayas it is called
the Yeti, or Abominable Snowman. In the Pacific
Northwest it is called Sasquatch, or Bigfoot. Are these
creatures real? Probably not, but who knows?

Chapter 31 • *Grey Goo*

Nanotechnology is real, but we're still a long
way from self-replicating mole-removing nanobots.
As for "grey goo," who knows? Science!

Chapter 35 •
Computer-assisted hydrogen-fiber waldoes

Waldoes are mechanical "hands" controlled
by a human operator moving his or her real hands.
Waldoes were first described and named by sci-fi
writer Robert Heinlein back in 1942. Today the term

waldo is sometimes used to describe many types of remote-control devices, such as those used in micro-surgery. But waldoes small enough to manipulate molecules do not exist . . . yet. Science!

Chapter 42 • *Infrasonics*

Whales and elephants and other animals really do communicate using low frequency sounds that humans can't hear, and there is evidence that such sounds cause anxiety and discomfort in humans, even though they are not consciously perceived. Science!

Chapter 47 • *The Flinkwater Factor*

When a bunch of smart, geeky people get together, lots of smart, geeky things happen. It happened during the Manhattan Project in the 1940s, and it's happening right now at Apple, Google, and other high-tech companies. Science!

Turn the page
for a sneak peek at
Ginger Crump's next misadventure
in *The Forgetting Machine*

Dead Trees

I found my dad in his study with his nose in a book made out of dead trees. Dad can be embarrassingly retro at times. A *lot* of the times, actually. Like every day. I mean, who reads *paper* books anymore?

Dad has more paper books than he has hairs on his head. Not that he has that many hairs anymore. But still . . . a lot of books. His entire study is lined with the nasty papery things.

He was reading something called *The Island of Dr. Moreau*. I wondered why a doctor would want to live on an island, but I'd learned to never ask my father about *any* book *ever*—a simple polite inquiry was likely to turn into a fifteen-minute lecture.

I took a deep breath and said, "Dad, why is our town called Flinkwater?"

He frowned and shrugged. "Because of the *flink* in the *water*?"

"Dad!"

"Maybe flink is some sort of fish, Ginger. I wouldn't know." One of my father's many quirks is that he hates fish. He won't even eat a tuna sandwich.

"There's no such word as 'flink,'" I said. "I looked it up."

He sighed and closed the book over his index finger to keep his place. If he'd been reading on his tablet, he wouldn't have that problem.

"Why do you ask, Ginger?"

"It's for this stupid school report."

"Maybe the town was founded by somebody named Flinkwater." He shrugged. "I really couldn't say."

"But . . . you're supposed know everything!"

"Apparently I don't," he said.

"Isn't your finger getting squished?"

"A little bit," he said, flipping open the book to ease the pressure.

"How come you don't just read on your tab?"

In my not-so-humble opinion, a proper book should be represented by an icon on a screen. Printing books on paper is as primitive as wearing animal skins or recording music on a plastic disk. Paper books won't let you make the font bigger or smaller, they aren't illuminated, and there's no search function. Also, they take up a lot of space, and they are heavy, unsanitary, unsightly, and noisy—the sound of someone flipping through those dry, whispery pages sets my teeth on edge.

"Studies have shown that reading paper books results in greater memory retention," he said.

"*I* don't have any problem remembering," I said.

"Well, I certainly do. I didn't grow up with e-books. When I was your age, we were still reading on stone tablets."

"Dad!"

He laughed. "Okay, we did have e-books, but they were pretty primitive. Anyway, I'm not taking any chances, what with all the forgetting going on these days,"

"All what forgetting?" I asked.

"Several of our people at ACPOD have been experiencing abnormal memory loss," he said. "It's become an epidemic. Just yesterday one of our engineers asked me my name, and he's been working with me for the past ten years."

ACPOD, in case you've been living under a rock for your entire life, is the world's largest manufacturer of Articulated Computerized Peripheral Devices. If you own a robot, it probably came from Flinkwater, Iowa. My parents—along with half the adult population of Flinkwater—work at ACPOD.

"Fortunately, one of our neuroprosthetics experts, Ernie Rausch, has developed an experimental memorization technique that is quite remarkable. He gave me a demonstration, and I now know all fourteen hundred lines of Longfellow's poem 'Evangeline.'"

"That's a lot of lines," I said. "How did you do it?"

"The funny thing is, I don't remember! One minute I was in the neuroprosthetics lab, and the next thing I knew I was back at my desk with my head full of Longfellow. And I couldn't remember my ACPOD password."

"It's Mom's maiden name backward, plus the first seven digits of pi," I said.

He gave me a sharp look. "How do you know that?"

I pointed at the sticky note on the corner of his computer display, where he had written *KNUF3.141592*—not exactly the best way to keep your secret password secret.

"Oh, yeah," he said. "Like I said, my memory has been playing tricks on me."

"And you think reading books printed on pulverized wood pulp is the answer?"

"I guess I just prefer *real* books," he said.

I like books too. But I read them on my tablet. Like a normal person.

"Think of all the trees they had to cut down to make the paper," I said.

"Yes, but how many *prehistoric* trees do you think it took to make the crude oil used to make the plastic case for your tablet?"

"Oil doesn't come from trees," I said. "It comes from hundred-million-year-old algae."

He laughed. "Apparently that 'stupid school' is teaching you something. As for the origin of Flinkwater, your mother has lived here her whole life. Ask her."

Before I go on—and I *can* go on—I should introduce myself.

Presenting the fabulous Guinevere Crump—recently turned fourteen, speller of difficult words, defender of helpless animals, fiancée of the smartest boy in the universe, problem solver extraordinaire, revolutionary rabble-rouser, social-justice crusader, and ravishing red-haired beauty—at your service. You may call me Ginger, or on formal occasions, Your Majesty.

So there. I'm glad we got that out of the way.

"Ask your father," said my mother.

"He told me to ask *you*! Your family has been here forever, right? You can't answer a simple question?"

She shot me her glittery, narrow-eyed witch queen look. "Ginger, if it's so simple, why do you ask?"

My mother doesn't scare me. Usually. But she tries.

"It's for school."

"Look it up."

"I tried," I said. Which wasn't completely true. Actually, I'd thought it would be easier to just ask. My mistake. "Do you even *know*?"

"Of course I *know*. I've lived here my entire life. But I'm sure you can figure it out on your own."

"I'm trying to figure it out by asking you."

"Ginger, I'm not going to do your homework for you. I'm busy." She went back to her oh-so-important task: trying to reprogram our DustBot swarm by stabbing at the DustBot control module with her red-nailed fingers. She didn't think the bots were doing a good enough job sucking Barney's cat hair off the carpet. It's Barney's fault. He keeps flipping the bots onto their backs, leaving them to buzz and spin around until somebody turns them right side up.

She might have better luck reprogramming the cat.

"If I get an F, it'll be your fault," I said.

She lowered the control module and gave me a look that was supposed to freeze the blood in my veins. I countered with my wide-eyed-innocent look. It was a mother-daughter standoff.

"Ask your school librarian," she said after a moment.

"Mom, it's Saturday. No school. And next week we get off Monday and Tuesday for teachers' conferences. And my report is due Wednesday."

She arched one precisely plucked eyebrow. "Then you'll just have to go to Flinkwater Memorial."

I was afraid she'd say that.

Did you LOVE reading this book?

Visit the Whyville...

Where you can:

◯ Discover great books!

◯ Meet new friends!

◯ Read exclusive sneak peeks and more!

Log on to visit now!
bookhive.whyville.net

"You're a tracker, Jack Buckles,
like your father and his father
before him. . . ."

In his middle-grade debut, James R. Hannibal
takes readers on a thrilling adventure through history—
with a touch of English magic.

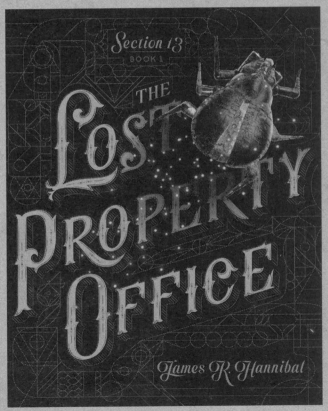

KENNETH OPPEL'S *THE NEST*
is a five-star eerie masterpiece.

★ "With subtle, spine-chilling horror at its heart, this tale of triumph over monsters—both outside and in—is outstanding."—*Booklist*, starred review

★ "Compelling and accessible."—*Kirkus Reviews*, starred review

★ "Oppel uses a dark and disturbing lens to produce an unnerving psychological thriller."—*Publishers Weekly*, starred review

★ "Emotionally haunting. . . . Recommended as a first purchase." —*School Library Journal*, starred review

★ "A tight and focused story about the dangers of wishing things back to normal at any cost. . . . The emotional resonance is deep, and Steve's precarious interactions with the honey-voiced queen make one's skin crawl." —*Horn Book*, starred review